"I need to understand what happened."

Alissa paused, gathering her thoughts. "I know it sounds crazy, but I feel a connection to them. They were happy here once. I feel like I owe it to them to bring that happiness back."

"You already have," Danny said.

She glanced at him, but his face was turned away, looking up at the maple leaves that hung above them. This was the closest he'd come to revealing any feelings for her. She could ask him what he meant. Find out if he thought of her as someone more than the person who signed his paychecks.

Or she could let the moment pass.

Continue living a life without complications.

Dear Reader,

I've always been fascinated by historic homes. As I walk the halls, I like to imagine the previous owners taking those same steps. What were their lives like? Were they happy here? While I don't believe in ghosts in the stereotypical, chain-rattling sense, I've often wondered if a home's past owners leave some trace of themselves behind. That curiosity was the inspiration for *The House of Secrets*.

By tracing the story of two women—Evelyn Brewster in the early 1900s and Alissa Franklin in the present—I wanted to explore how two seemingly different lives can share certain parallels. As a history buff, I believe we can all learn from the past—and if you can solve a long-buried mystery along the way, all the better!

Thanks for following along.

Happy reading!

Elizabeth Blackwell

THE HOUSE OF SECRETS
Elizabeth Blackwell

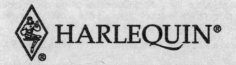

HARLEQUIN®

TORONTO • NEW YORK • LONDON
AMSTERDAM • PARIS • SYDNEY • HAMBURG
STOCKHOLM • ATHENS • TOKYO • MILAN • MADRID
PRAGUE • WARSAW • BUDAPEST • AUCKLAND

Recycling programs
for this product may
not exist in your area.

ISBN-13: 978-0-373-71559-6
ISBN-10: 0-373-71559-5

THE HOUSE OF SECRETS

Copyright © 2009 by Elizabeth Blackwell.

This edition published by arrangement with Harlequin Books S.A.

www.eHarlequin.com

Printed in U.S.A.

ABOUT THE AUTHOR

As a magazine writer and editor, Elizabeth Blackwell has written about everything from designing a dream kitchen to fighting a duel. She lives outside Chicago with her husband, daughter, twin boys and a vast collection of long underwear. Her first novel, *The Letter,* won first prize in eHarlequin.com's epic romance contest and was published by Harlequin Everlasting Love in 2007. *The House of Secrets* is her first Harlequin Superromance book.

Books by Elizabeth Blackwell

HARLEQUIN EVERLASTING LOVE
11—THE LETTER

To Robert, a wonderful handyman
and even better husband

CHAPTER ONE

"I LOVE IT."

It was ridiculous, this sudden desire Alissa Franklin felt for the dilapidated old house. It was far too big for one person: six bedrooms, a huge dining room, a formal parlor the size of a ballroom. It was also a good thirty miles from her office in downtown Baltimore, which would mean a nightmare commute. Not to mention the building's shabby condition—sagging front stairs, paint peeling off the siding, scrapes marring the wood floors and water damage on some of the upstairs ceilings. It must have been beautiful once, a classic wood-frame Queen Anne with a wide front porch and oversized windows that welcomed the sunlight. Now, the elegant silhouette was all that remained of its past glory.

But as Alissa walked through the rooms and stared at the overgrown garden in back, she felt she belonged. She imagined the gloomy spaces transformed by fresh coats of paint and new curtains. The power of the vision was so strong that she turned to Brad before they had even left the second floor. "I love it," she whispered.

Brad gave her the look he always did when confronted with one of her spontaneous enthusiasms. His mouth curved in a half scowl, his scornful dark eyes piercing her. Once, that look had been able to stun her into silence. Now, after four years of on-again, off-again dating, it only irritated her. It had lost its power.

"Shh," Brad whispered, nodding his head toward the Realtor walking a few steps ahead of them.

Alissa followed Brad up to the third floor, where the servants' quarters were crammed under the roof's sloping eaves. Although now nearly empty, the rooms were a testament to a time when this was a vibrant home, bustling with life. Through a tiny window, Alissa looked out over the town of Oak Hill, spread out below her. The servants may have been stuck in the smallest, stuffiest rooms, but they'd had the best view.

Alissa moved silently behind Brad and the Realtor as they descended the narrow stairs to the second floor, then along the grand staircase that wound down to the foyer. An elaborate cut-glass chandelier—hazy under a layer of dust—signaled that this was a space designed to impress, even intimidate. Alissa imagined someone from town arriving here, climbing out of a carriage on the circular drive, walking through the entrance and being confronted with this foyer. Taking in the glittering chandelier, the marble floor and the statues that would have been displayed in the now-vacant wall recesses. The people who lived in the simple brick houses of the town would have been dumbstruck by the scale of this mansion. Yet despite its opulence, the place still felt like a home, somewhere Alissa could see herself living.

"So?" the Realtor asked. She was a tall, slim woman who obviously took pride in her appearance, from the ash-blond hair swept into a sleek chignon to her immaculate black patent-leather heels. Her highlights and expertly applied makeup camouflaged her age, which could have been anywhere from forty to sixty. When Alissa had called the phone number on the For Sale sign in front of the house—"Let's just take a peek," she'd told Brad, pulling her cell phone from her purse—the Realtor had answered on the second ring and offered to show them the place immediately.

"I live only a few houses away," she'd said. "It's no trouble."

Brad had protested, of course, saying he didn't want to be driving the country roads after dark. But Alissa knew the real reason behind his impatience. After what was supposed to be a romantic weekend getaway—a last-ditch attempt to smooth over the fault lines in their relationship—Brad was ready to give up the pretense of being a happy couple. Touring this house would only postpone the inevitable, awkward conversation about their future. Perhaps delaying that moment was what made Alissa so anxious to see the house.

The Realtor introduced herself as Elaine Price, and Alissa explained that she was an interior designer interested in historic homes.

"I'd be happy to show you around," Elaine said as she led them up the front steps. "It's quite a treasure."

Brad had scowled as he took in the state of the house, which clearly hadn't been lived in for years. Elaine led them briskly along, showing each room with a minimum of description, as if the tall ceilings and generous spaces could speak for themselves. Now she stood before them in the foyer, smiling graciously.

"So?"

Alissa heard Brad starting to speak. "Well, if that's

it…" But she wasn't ready to leave. She needed more time here, time to savor the atmosphere of this magical place.

"When was the house built?" Alissa asked.

"It's more than a hundred years old—1904, I think. It was built for a young married couple." Elaine smiled, continuing in a softer tone, "It's actually a very romantic story."

Alissa kept her eyes focused on Elaine, ignoring Brad's impatient sigh.

"You've heard of the Brewsters?" Elaine asked, leading them out the front door. The late-afternoon sun sent their shadows sprawling down the wide steps and circular gravel driveway. Alissa shook her head.

"There aren't any left, at least around here, but they used to be the richest family in the area," Elaine said. "Made their money in shipping. Do you know Brewster Street near the harbor in Baltimore?"

Alissa nodded. "Yes, my dentist's office is there."

"That street was named for them," said Elaine. "Sometime in the mid-nineteenth century, the family built an enormous country estate, which became their main residence. The city was filthy back then, and the air was supposed to be healthier out here. Which it still is, no doubt!"

Brad nodded politely, but Alissa could tell he was anxious to speed things along.

"So, is this where the family lived?" she asked.

"Oh, no. They had a far grander home about half a mile that way." Elaine gestured beyond the backyard. "It was one of those sprawling Gothic manors that seem to stretch on for miles. It was demolished in the sixties to make room for the highway. A tragic architectural loss, but the house was completely impractical for modern families."

Elaine paused, then gestured back toward the existing house's facade. "This was built for Mr. Charles Brewster, the eldest son of Edward Brewster, who built the original estate. Edward had three children, and homes were to be built for each of them on the property once they were married. Charles was one of the wealthiest, most eligible bachelors in the county. But when it came time to get married, he chose the daughter of his mother's dressmaker. It was *quite* the scandal."

"She must have been very special," Alissa said.

"Her name was Evelyn," Elaine continued. "Apparently she was very lovely. Educated as well, which was unusual for someone from a working-class family. Charles's mother fought the match, but they were simply too much in love. It was a whirlwind courtship, and Charles had workers here day and night to finish the house for his bride. I've always thought of this place as his wedding gift to her."

"And they lived happily ever after, right?" Alissa said.

Elaine shook her head quickly. "I'm afraid not. Charles died only a year later, and Evelyn moved away. The memories were simply too painful. The house eventually passed out of the family. For the past thirty years or so, it's been owned by Mrs. Foster, who lived here first with her husband, then, when he died, with her sister. After a while, though, it became too much to keep up on their own. A house like this needs a fair bit of maintenance."

From what Alissa could see, the two sisters hadn't been able to keep up with the house for some time.

"How long has the house been empty?" Brad asked.

Elaine adjusted her necklace, avoiding his eyes. "A few years."

"How many, exactly?"

"Oh, about three."

"And it's been on the market since then?" Brad asked. This, he seemed to imply, was the kiss of death for real estate.

"Oh, off and on," Elaine said vaguely. "The family considered renovating, then thought they'd try to find a buyer as is—so many people prefer to do their own updating. There have been some offers, mostly from developers looking to tear it down. The family would prefer to see the home remain intact, so they're waiting for that special person who sees its potential." She gave Alissa a hopeful smile.

"Well, thank you for showing us around," said Brad, reaching out to shake Elaine's hand. "We've got your card if we have any questions." He walked swiftly down the steps and started along the driveway.

Alissa hung back. "You didn't tell us the price," she reminded the Realtor.

Elaine smiled. "Well, as I said, the family is looking for someone who appreciates the historic nature of the home. For the right person, I believe they'd be willing to be flexible." She named a figure so absurdly low— a number not much higher than the price Alissa had paid for her condo a few years before—that Alissa let out a shocked laugh.

"You're kidding," she said.

Elaine lowered her voice and leaned in closer. "This isn't an easy house to sell," she confided. "The family doesn't need the money. If they did, they would've sold to the developers. They have a sentimental attachment to the house, and I know they're happy to make accommodations for someone who truly cares for the place."

Alissa glanced at Brad, who was already standing by the gate at the end of the long driveway. He jingled his car keys impatiently.

"Thank you," Alissa said, shaking Elaine's hand. "It's a wonderful house."

"It's just waiting for a nice young family," Elaine said with a wink.

"Oh, we're not married," Alissa protested. For years, she had halfheartedly daydreamed about standing at an altar, saying "I do" to Brad. Those fantasies had gradually faded.

"So sorry," Elaine said with the practiced grace of someone used to extracting herself from awkward situations. "Well, I can see you're in a hurry. Do call if you have any questions."

"Yes, I will." Alissa scurried down the driveway and nudged Brad forward with one hand. "Okay, we can go now."

As they drove off, Alissa stole one last glimpse at what she already thought of as the Brewster house. She imagined herself as a young bride, being carried over the threshold by a man who had risked everything to marry her. Their house must have been a refuge from a disapproving world. What would it be like to be so in love that you were willing to defy your family and break all the rules?

Alissa had always had an active imagination. It was the key to her professional success. Being an interior designer took more than sorting through paint chips and fabric samples; it took a talent for envisioning a space as it should be, not as it was, then convincing clients that she could make it happen. As soon as she was old enough to hold a paintbrush, Alissa had begged her mother to let her paint her room. By her teens, she was sewing slip-covers for the living-room furniture and making her own bedspreads. Bringing the Brewster house back to life would be the ultimate test of her talent.

Brad eyed her from the driver's seat. "That place looked cool from the outside, but c'mon—it was a dump."

Alissa felt her shoulders tense. "It just needs some work," she said.

"And you think you can save it?" Brad asked. "You'd go bankrupt."

"There's the money from my mom…" Alissa began, then stopped. The money her mother had left when she died of cancer a year ago, which she'd told Alissa to use to "follow her dreams." Alissa had assumed she'd put it toward a wedding, a fairy-tale affair so magical it might make up for her mother's absence. Clearly that wasn't likely now, given the state of her relationship with Brad. Had her mother hoped for something else?

"Besides," Alissa continued after a moment, "wanna guess the asking price?"

Brad perked up with surprise when she told him. "Really?"

"Yeah," Alissa said. "Plus, Elaine more or less said they'd be willing to drop the price even lower for the right person. If I sold my condo and took out a loan, I might have enough for renovations. I could get fabric and furniture from some of the firm's suppliers at cost, so I'd be saving a ton of money there…."

"Hang on. You took one tour of the house and now you're selling your condo?" Brad asked. He didn't bother to hide his disbelief.

"I said *if,*" Alissa protested. But in her heart, she had already let go of the downtown loft, with its exposed-brick walls and stainless-steel kitchen. She saw herself at the Brewster house, stripping the paint off the elaborate crown molding in that beautiful parlor, or washing the streaked windows so the sun could shine in once again.

"The commute would be awful," Brad said.

"I know." Already, Alissa dreaded going to the office each day; a long drive would only give her more time to be miserable. Maureen, her boss, hovered over her as if she were still an intern, even though she had been a licensed designer for nearly three years. Now that clients had started specifically requesting Alissa, Maureen had become even more competitive and distrusting. If Alissa moved out to Oak Hill, maybe she could arrange to go to the office only part-time.

Or better yet, not go in at all. For years, Alissa had dreamed of running her own business. Finally working the way she wanted to, without the distraction of a temperamental boss. It was impossible, of course—there was no way she could buy a massive house *and* quit her job. It would be crazy. And yet, Alissa felt a stirring of excitement at the prospect. The Brewster house, which had captured her imagination despite its neglected condition, now seemed like the key to a whole new life.

Brad laughed sarcastically. "I can't believe you were seriously thinking of buying that place," he said.

I still am, Alissa thought. But she remained silent.

They drove on, the sound of the humming wheels mesmerizing them until they drifted into their own thoughts. In the end, it was Brad who spoke first. His ability to cut to the truth was one quality she still admired about him.

"So this is it, huh?" he said, keeping his eyes fixed on the road ahead.

Alissa started to ask him what he meant, then stopped herself. What was the point? Their passion for each other—once so exciting, so all-consuming—had fizzled in the face of their ultimate incompatibility. Brad was a good-time guy who wanted to keep the party going even as he passed thirty; Alissa was happiest cocooning at home and getting to bed before midnight. Brad liked hot summer nights and tropical beaches; Alissa preferred cool fall afternoons and vacations at mountaintop lodges. It was no one's fault. They should be able to say goodbye without regret. Still, Alissa didn't want to make the final decision.

"Are you calling it quits?" Alissa asked.

"Don't put this on me," said Brad, still gazing at the darkening road. "You've wanted out for a long time. Why else do you think you got so worked up about that old house?"

As their conversation continued, reaching its unavoidable conclusion, they both remained calm and detached. Later, thinking back on that drive, Alissa was amazed by how effortlessly her future with Brad slipped away.

"I'll come by after work tomorrow to pick up my things," Brad said as he pulled the car up in front of her building. "If that's all right with you."

"Sure," said Alissa. There was nothing left to say, so she got out, closed the door and walked inside without looking back.

Once inside, she walked around the condo, looking for evidence of Brad that would have to be cleared out. Considering how long they had dated, he hadn't left much of a mark. A few framed pictures on a bookshelf. His college sweatshirt lying over the arm of the couch. The extra toothbrush she had bought for him, lying next to hers on the side of her bathroom sink. Erasing him from her life would only take a few minutes. It wasn't supposed to be so easy, was it?

Logically, Alissa knew they had done the right thing. But she couldn't relax, couldn't concentrate. The stark, gleaming metals and thickly varnished wood surrounding her felt cold and unwelcoming. She had been inspired by contemporary design when she'd decorated her home, determined to make it feel clean and modern. But after touring the Brewster house, the space felt soulless.

Alissa flashed back to the day she started at design school. How she had rushed home that night to call her parents, giddily describing the projects she would be working on that semester. She had tried to recapture that joy many times in the following years, etching that love of her work into her brain so it wouldn't be forgotten among the day-to-day frustrations of Maureen's disapproval. But now, thinking about the Brewster house, Alissa felt a flash of excitement that echoed that first day of class. She let the feeling wash over her. *I'll buy it,* she decided, *and I will be happy there.*

CHAPTER TWO

1904

EVELYN O'KEEFE'S wedding day passed in a blur. For years afterward, only one image remained clear: the sight of Will Brewster pulling up in front of the church in his lurching, dirt-spattered motorcar, exuding such vitality that everyone else seemed to fade into the background. Evelyn had never believed in love at first sight. The idea of losing her heart to someone she had just met—on her wedding day, no less—had always struck her as absurd. But from the moment Will arrived, she couldn't stop watching him. He stepped easily from the car and greeted the guests mingling around him. His smile dazzled her as he pulled up his goggles and caught her eye. The attraction was instantaneous.

Until that point, the wedding and reception had progressed as smoothly as any other social event held at the Brewster estate. Alma Brewster, her new mother-in-law, had made all the arrangements. It was never suggested that Evelyn be involved in the planning. Alma knew what food was appropriate for the sit-down dinner and which flowers would be in season. Since Alma was paying for everything and hosting the reception in her home, Evelyn acquiesced immediately. It was a relief to be spared potential social disaster.

The only decision Evelyn made was the style of her wedding dress, which was sewn by her mother, Katherine. Evelyn's earliest memories were of Katherine holding a needle, with a pincushion and scissors tucked into a white apron wrapped around her waist. Even when Evelyn's father, Thomas, was alive and Katherine spent most days helping him at the family's general store, she'd always had fabric and needles tucked behind the counter, waiting for a lull. When Thomas died and they were forced to sell the store to cover unexpected bills and debts, Katherine refused to despair. "We'll get by," she told Evelyn. "I always have my sewing."

And so, Katherine had transformed herself from meek assistant to breadwinner, eventually becoming the dressmaker to many of Chesapeake County's richest families. And it had all begun with a wedding. Evelyn could still remember the day Katherine had flung open the front door and shouted for her.

"What is it? What's happened?" Evelyn asked breathlessly as she raced down the stairs, bracing herself for bad news. Though only sixteen, she had none of the naive hopefulness common among girls her age. Already, life had taught her to be wary of change.

"Lavinia Brewster's getting married," Katherine announced. "Mabel Goodridge and two other ladies have already asked me to make dresses for them, and I'm sure there will be more to come. If they like my work, they'll hire me again, I just know it. Thank heavens for the Brewsters!"

The Brewsters. The richest family in Oak Hill. The ones who set the tone for everyone else to follow. If Alma Brewster, the matriarch, wore purple ostrich plumes in her hat at church, the rest of the women in town scrambled to find purple feathers for the next week. The lives of her three children were tracked and discussed as if they were royalty. William, the eldest, known as the family ne'er-do-well, had been shipped off to boarding school at a young age and was now reportedly doing his best to squander his allowance in Europe. Charles, the middle child, was the heir apparent. After graduating from Harvard University and spending a year in London, he was being groomed as the future leader of Brewster Shipping. Their younger sister, Lavinia, had been given a lavish coming-out ball in Baltimore and had dazzled her way through cotillions and debutante dances in New York and Paris.

Now Lavinia was getting married. Half the women invited to the wedding hired Katherine to make their dresses. Although it meant working well into the night for weeks, the money earned from that one event brought Evelyn one step closer to her dream of going to college.

Thanks to Lavinia Brewster's wedding, Katherine was able to set aside enough money for Evelyn to enroll in a teacher-training program when she was eighteen. Over the next five years, she continued her studies in fits and starts, completing courses whenever she had earned enough money tutoring the spoiled children of rich Baltimore families. During visits home, Katherine would update her on the local gossip, usually dominated by news of the Brewsters: William hadn't come home for his father's funeral, Lavinia had given birth to a baby girl. To Evelyn, the Brewsters seemed more like legendary figures than real people. Until the day she was summoned to their mansion on the hill. The place where her life changed forever.

It was a few months after she had received her teaching degree. Evelyn was accompanying her mother to a meeting of their church's Bible study group, which usually focused more on gossip than Gospel. She had recently received an offer to teach at a private girls' school in Philadelphia. The salary was tempting, but Evelyn was torn at the thought of leaving her mother. As the two women walked through town, Evelyn was distracted by the decision she faced. Then a carriage clattered past and stopped suddenly just a few steps ahead of them.

"That's Mrs. Brewster," Katherine noted, walking quickly toward the carriage.

As they approached, an elegant older woman leaned out a side window. An enormous plumed hat only partially obscured her high forehead. She held her neck and shoulders rigid, as if to counteract the drooping skin around her chin and eyes. Her thin lips curved in a perfect half-moon of a smile, but her deep blue eyes held no trace of warmth.

"Mrs. O'Keefe," she said.

"Mrs. Brewster." Katherine tilted her head in submission. "Allow me to introduce my daughter, Evelyn."

Evelyn started to bow, but quickly pulled herself upright. It was bad enough that her mother was acting like a servant.

"You're the one attending the ladies' college?" Mrs.

Brewster asked, her soothing voice at odds with the stiffness of her posture.

"Yes," Katherine confirmed. "Evelyn received her degree in June. She was the top-ranked student in her class."

Mrs. Brewster stared at Evelyn intently. "Do you plan to pursue teaching?"

"Yes, I'm considering an offer in Philadelphia."

Mrs. Brewster nodded thoughtfully. "Lavinia's daughter, Beatrice, has just turned six, and she's beyond the capabilities of her nanny," she said. "We shall have a proper English governess once she is older, of course, but for the next few years she needs someone to teach her writing and comportment and that sort of thing." She raised her shoulders slightly in a hint of a shrug. "If you're free Friday morning, we can discuss the position in further detail." It was phrased as an invitation, but Alma's tone made it clear she wasn't used to being denied.

"Thank you so much," Katherine gushed, filling the void of Evelyn's silence. "She can be there at whatever time is convenient."

"We'll say ten o'clock sharp," Mrs. Brewster declared. "See Hayes at the front entrance when you arrive."

Katherine thanked her effusively, but Evelyn said nothing as Mrs. Brewster slid the carriage window shut and drove away.

Katherine grabbed Evelyn's arm and pulled her daughter close.

"Oh, darling, how wonderful!" she exclaimed. "Imagine, a position with the Brewsters!"

"Until the real English governess arrives," Evelyn said.

"You can't possibly take offense at that!" Katherine scolded with a gentle slap to Evelyn's arm. "Besides, you weren't planning on working more than a few years, were you? After you earn some money, you'll want to think about getting married."

"I suppose," said Evelyn.

"And she wants you to come to the front entrance," Katherine gushed. "That's a very good sign. When I started doing alterations for her, I had to use the servants' entrance. It was years before I was welcome at the front door."

"No matter which door I walk through, I'll still be a servant," Evelyn said, not bothering to hide her irritation.

"Have those professors at school been filling your head with socialist nonsense?" Katherine scoffed. "The Brewsters' money has supported us through difficult times, as you should know. Mrs. Brewster deserves the courtesy of your consideration."

"Yes, Mother," Evelyn said.

"I know she seems high-and-mighty, but that's just her manner. Besides, if you're Lavinia's daughter's governess, you'll hardly see Mrs. Brewster. Lavinia has her own home on the estate."

"Then why is Mrs. Brewster arranging the interviews?" Evelyn asked. To that, Katherine had no answer.

In the days before the interview, Evelyn came up with a plan. The more she thought about the position in Philadelphia, the more appealing the offer became. This could be her chance to make a mark on the world by teaching young girls to value themselves and their intelligence. She could still visit her mother every weekend. Katherine might even be convinced to move to Philadelphia with her.

But she couldn't insult the Brewsters. The key was to make sure Alma Brewster didn't want to hire her. She could accomplish that by being herself: independent and outspoken. She would not beg for the position, and she would not cater to Alma Brewster's snobbishness. Mrs. Brewster would dismiss her, and that would be that.

It was only when the butler Hayes—his rotund body waddling on two thin legs like Humpty Dumpty brought to life—led Evelyn into what he called the morning room, that her self-confidence faltered. She had prepared herself to stand up to Alma Brewster. But she hadn't expected to be faced with a roomful of people, all eying her curiously as she entered.

Mrs. Brewster immediately took charge.

"Miss O'Keefe, I appreciate your promptness," she said. "I am often appalled by the tardiness of people your age. Please, come in. I will make the introductions." She led Evelyn toward a pale, nervous-looking young woman clutching the hand of a small girl whose flushed face was surrounded by tangled blond ringlets.

"This is my daughter, Lavinia Preston, and my granddaughter, Beatrice." Lavinia nodded at Evelyn, while Beatrice stared at her resentfully.

"Beatrice was attempting to hurl herself into the garden fountain a few moments ago," Alma said. "It is precisely this willfulness we need to remedy. Isn't that right, Lavinia?"

Lavinia nodded again, but still said nothing.

"This is Beatrice's father, Winslow Preston," Mrs. Brewster said, indicating a middle-aged man with a bloated stomach that strained against his waistcoat. He bent his head and shoulders quickly in a brief acknowledgment of Evelyn's presence.

"And, of course, Charles," Mrs. Brewster added, as if the other person in the room needed no introduction.

Charles Brewster was a favorite subject of local gossip. Nearly thirty and still a bachelor, his marriage plans were the topic of endless speculation. His wealth and status put the most prestigious possibilities within reach. But for all the discussions of his money, his social connections and his talent for business, Evelyn had never realized how handsome he was until now. He had his mother's erect posture, but what came across as snobbish in Mrs. Brewster made him appear dignified. His dark brown hair was combed carefully back from his forehead, not a lock out of place. A moustache was neatly trimmed. His deep blue eyes focused on Evelyn, observing everything about her but giving nothing away.

"A pleasure to meet you, Miss O'Keefe," he said smoothly, tipping his head. "Mother, if you intend on a lengthy interrogation…"

Mrs. Brewster silenced him with a wave of her hand. "If Miss O'Keefe is to become a member of this household, I expect you to show an interest. Your business affairs can wait." She turned back to Evelyn. "Come—sit down."

Evelyn watched as the family members took their places along two parallel sofas in the center of the room: the Prestons on one side, Mrs. Brewster and Charles on the other. After a moment's hesitation, Evelyn settled on a narrow wooden chair.

Mrs. Brewster began by quizzing Evelyn about her education and her qualifications, nodding approvingly when she mentioned the Baltimore families she had worked for. Beatrice sulked, Winslow looked bored and Lavinia watched silently. But it was Charles who unnerved Evelyn the most. For someone who had tried to avoid the interview, he appeared surprisingly interested in Evelyn's answers.

"I'm curious," he interrupted. "What is your philosophy on education for women?"

Evelyn smiled. "I believe women should receive as much education as possible."

"But if every respectable woman's goal is marriage," Charles continued, "why the need for any education? Beyond the simple requirements of literacy and perhaps familiarity with household finances."

"I believe a successful marriage is one between intellectual equals," Evelyn responded, echoing a sentiment that had often been debated at college. "A husband will grow bored with a silly wife, but an educated woman is a worthy companion for life."

"Hmph," Mrs. Brewster snorted. "Do you think all young ladies should renounce marriage and family to attend college?"

Her face flushed, Evelyn rose to the bait. "Of course not," she said quickly. "However—and with no offense intended—women used to be considered educated if they had a few years of French and could play a waltz on the piano. We have now entered a new century. Times have changed."

"Indeed they have," Charles agreed. To Evelyn's surprise, he looked pleased.

"I certainly wish Beatrice to have every opportunity," Mrs. Brewster said. "College is not necessary for someone in her position, but I can see how it would be advantageous for a woman like you, who has to make her own way in the world."

Evelyn nodded, fairly certain she'd been insulted.

"Now, do you have any questions?" Mrs. Brewster asked.

Evelyn remembered Mrs. Brewster's offhand comment about her becoming part of the household. "Is this a live-in position?" she asked. If so, she wouldn't hesitate to decline. Being surrounded by these people every day would be intolerable.

"Given that you live in town, a daily schedule could be arranged," Mrs. Brewster said. "I see no need to deprive your mother of your company. I know all too well what it is to be a widow alone in this world."

Hardly alone, thought Evelyn, with three children and a household full of staff.

"I assume lessons would be held at Mr. and Mrs. Preston's home?"

Mrs. Brewster shook her head. "We have a proper schoolroom here," she said. "My own children took their lessons there. It's fully supplied, but there will be funds set aside for books and any other necessities that may be required. Well then," Mrs. Brewster continued, rising to her feet. "That will be all. We have a few other candidates expected today, but we hope to make a speedy decision. It's high time Beatrice's wild ways were tamed."

"Yes, of course. Thank you for considering me." Evelyn said her goodbyes quickly and almost raced out of the room. How foolish she had been, thinking that *she* would reject the Brewsters! Of course they would interview other governesses, all of them more experienced and more sophisticated than her. This meeting was simply a gesture of goodwill toward her mother, a gracious signal to the town that the Brewsters weren't above hiring locals on occasion.

In her hurry to leave the house, Evelyn dashed toward the front door, barely giving Hayes the chance to open it for her. As she made her way swiftly down the drive, she heard her name being shouted behind her. "Miss O'Keefe!"

She stopped and turned, stunned to see Charles Brewster taking the front steps two at a time.

"Your hat, Miss O'Keefe!"

He held up Evelyn's best hat, made of dark blue straw and decorated with a ring of woven white ribbons. Against the backdrop of the Brewster mansion, it now appeared worn and faded.

"Oh, thank you," Evelyn muttered as she gingerly took the hat from his hands, careful that their fingers didn't touch.

"Hayes is far too corpulent to catch you, so I thought I'd try," he said.

"Yes." Evelyn was rarely at a loss for words, but she couldn't think of a thing to say. Especially since Charles, rather than turning back to the house, continued to stand in front of her, apparently waiting for something.

"Miss O'Keefe," he began, then coughed in an uncharacteristic display of nerves. "I hope I didn't offend you with my questioning. I'm afraid I may have been somewhat overbearing."

"Oh, not at all," Evelyn lied. "An educated woman— especially one who intends to teach children—should be able to defend her opinions."

"I couldn't agree more." He smiled reassuringly, and his voice softened. "Mother can be chilly, but she only wants what's best for the family. You acquitted yourself quite well."

"Thank you, Mr. Brewster." Once again, an awkward silence settled between them.

"It was a pleasure to meet you," Charles said finally, clasping her hand briefly with both of his. His touch sent a thrill of sensation up Evelyn's arm, and her heart began to pound. Then he was gone, back to his sprawling home, while Evelyn wondered if she had only imagined the question in his eyes.

WHEN MRS. BREWSTER OFFERED Evelyn the governess position, at double the salary she would have received in Philadelphia, Evelyn felt she had no choice but to accept. She began her duties warily, keeping to the schoolroom and avoiding her employer except when summoned to provide reports on Beatrice's progress. Yet most days, seemingly by chance, Evelyn found herself crossing paths with Charles. Gradually, she realized these encounters were no accident. Charles's tone moved from respectful to flirtatious, and Evelyn was flattered by his attention. There were moments stolen in the hallway of the Brewster mansion, his hand brushing hers as if by accident. Visits to the schoolroom as she tried unsuccessfully to concentrate on Beatrice. His whispered confession that she intrigued him as no other woman ever had. From then on, she was at his mercy.

At the time, she thought it was love. Why else would she weaken at the thought of his hand resting around her waist? It wasn't the grand romance she had once imagined—there were no intimate conversations or tender declarations of affection. Yet Charles had a hold over her that she had no wish to escape.

When Evelyn first confided the new developments to her mother, Katherine almost fainted with delight. She insisted on making new dresses for Evelyn and admonished her to be on her best behavior. When Charles finally appeared at the house one evening and asked for Evelyn's hand in marriage, Katherine could only nod and stammer before dissolving into tears of happiness.

The reaction at the Brewster home was considerably less joyful. When Charles brought Evelyn into the drawing room later that evening, announcing that she had accepted his proposal, Alma fixed her future daughter-in-law with an expression of such horror that Evelyn had to turn away.

"Nonsense," Alma declared after an agonizing silence.

Charles took a step toward his mother, his body stiff with self-righteous anger. "If you won't welcome my future wife, Mother, we are prepared to settle in Baltimore."

Alma eyed Evelyn up and down. "That won't be necessary. Charles, will you give us a moment alone, please?"

It took all of Evelyn's self-control to keep from clutching Charles's hand. Charles glanced at her, then back at his mother.

"Whatever you say to Evelyn, you can say in front of me."

"Very well." Alma paused, pacing in circles in front of them as if rounding up her thoughts. "Charles, if you are attempting to prove your independence, the point has been made. I urged you not to rush into marriage, yet you ignored my advice and proposed to someone who is utterly unsuitable." She turned to face Evelyn. "Miss O'Keefe, I am not unsympathetic. I understand your position, your family's precarious finances. You saw an opportunity with my son…"

"I assure you, I didn't," Evelyn protested. "Charles pursued me."

Alma glanced at Charles, taking in his amused smile. Then she smiled coldly at Evelyn.

"Very well," she conceded. "My son showed an interest, and you took advantage of it. No doubt you are quite skilled. I confess I was completely unaware of this turn of events. However, if you are willing to consider an alternate solution, I'm prepared to be quite generous."

"I have no interest in your money," Evelyn said. "Charles and I love each other."

Alma flinched.

"As you see, Mother, this is not a commercial transaction," said Charles, a note of contempt lurking beneath his cheerful words. "I have proposed, Evelyn has accepted, and we will be married. With or without your blessing."

Though Evelyn was heartened by Charles's resolve, she felt momentarily chilled by the fury in his eyes.

Alma nodded slowly. "If you are determined to go through with this, you will have it. Miss O'Keefe, may I offer my congratulations." But the words were a mere formality. Alma did not offer an embrace or even a handshake. Her body remained rigid, as if she were afraid she would crack into pieces if she moved.

"Don't worry, our house will be finished soon enough," Charles reassured Evelyn as they waited for the carriage to take her home. "You won't have to spend a night under this roof."

Their house. The thought of it was almost enough to distract Evelyn from the memory of Alma's insults. Construction had begun long before Charles's proposal to Evelyn, but she had been delighted by the building when he'd shown her around a few days before. She had never imagined a place so elegant could also feel so welcoming.

When the carriage arrived, Charles held the door open for Evelyn, then climbed in beside her. He closed the door behind him and drew her toward him for a kiss that obliterated her fears. Until now, Charles had given her nothing more than fleeting pecks on the cheek. Now, his lips explored her face in a frenzy of pent-up passion, his hands roaming along her shoulders and down her arms. Evelyn felt her body melt into his and wondered how she would manage to resist him until their wedding night.

It was only much later, as Evelyn lay in bed, that she felt a pang of doubt. She had told Alma that she and Charles were getting married because they loved each other. Yet Charles had never once told her so.

By the day of the wedding, however, any lingering worries about her future husband were overshadowed by the event itself. Evelyn moved through her duties as if in a dream. She glided down the aisle and repeated her vows in a firm but quiet voice. She smiled graciously as Charles escorted her back through the church and out the front doors.

Then she saw Will Brewster, and the haze lifted.

Charles hadn't expected his brother to come. Will had gone abroad years ago—"To study art," Alma had told Reverend Alderson's wife, in the same hushed tone she might have used to discuss a fatal illness. Charles had informed his brother about the wedding in a letter, but when no response arrived, Alma had crossed Will's name from the seating chart. Yet there he was, standing at the bottom of the church stairs, pulling off his grimy driving glasses and greeting Evelyn with a delighted smile.

"Will Brewster," he said cheerily, waving his hand. "I take it you're my new sister-in-law? Can I give you a lift to the reception?" Evelyn looked into his blue eyes, the same piercing shade as Charles's, but sparkling with an amusement she'd never seen from her husband. His dark blond hair was tousled from the drive, but despite his disheveled appearance, he held himself with the same strong confidence as the rest of his family. Evelyn couldn't help but smile back.

"A lift? In that monstrosity?" Charles asked incredulously.

"Nice to see you, too, Charles." Will laughed.

By this time, guests were filing out around them, and friends called out Will's name as they rushed up to greet him. It wasn't long before Alma pushed her way to the front. She hurried toward her eldest son, then stopped in her tracks when she saw the condition of his car and clothes.

"Oh, Will!" she admonished. "You look frightful!"

"There was no time to change," Will said. "I was trying not to miss the wedding—although apparently, I did anyway."

"Go to the house and clean up," Alma ordered. "We'll be serving dinner in one hour."

Will tipped his goggles in Evelyn's direction. "I'll look forward to getting acquainted this evening, Mrs. Brewster," he said. His voice had a light, teasing tone, as if acknowledging how ridiculous it was that she should now bear that name.

She meant to ask Charles about his brother, but she didn't have a chance. Three hundred guests had to make their way through the receiving line, then she and Charles had to be presented as man and wife and take their places at a table with Alma and an assortment of elderly Brewster relatives. Evelyn became aware of Will only later, after the dessert dishes had been cleared and the orchestra began playing. Evelyn looked at Charles expectantly, only to have him announce, "I never dance." There were so many things she didn't yet know about him.

A figure in an immaculately pressed tuxedo appeared at Evelyn's side.

"If my brother won't take his bride for a pass on the dance floor, perhaps I might be permitted the honor." Will's words were courteous to a fault, but Evelyn sensed an undercurrent of amusement.

Evelyn glanced at Charles, who waved her off. "Of course," he said, before continuing a discussion of trade tariffs with his great-uncle.

"Only Charles would discuss business during his wedding dinner," Will said, as he lightly took hold of Evelyn's waist and pulled her across the wood floor. "But I suppose you're used to that by now."

In truth, she wasn't. But revealing how little she really knew about Charles might seem disloyal. "The business keeps him very busy," she said.

"Oh, Charles was born an old man," Will said with a wink. "He's always been the serious one."

"And what are you?" Evelyn asked.

"Haven't you heard? I'm the black sheep."

Evelyn laughed, but she knew it was true. Charles seldom discussed his brother, and when he did, it was usually to criticize him.

"You're not at all what I expected," Will said. "When I heard Charles was marrying a governess, I pictured a humorless old spinster, the sort who used to rap my knuckles with a ruler when I misbehaved."

"Did that happen often?" Evelyn asked lightly.

"More than I care to admit." Will smiled, and Evelyn caught a glimpse of the boy he once was, his eyes twinkling with mischief, but without malice.

"You're not what I expected either," she admitted.

"Ah, now things get interesting," Will said, twirling her gently around the edge of the dance floor. "You imagined a clubfoot or some other deformity?"

Evelyn laughed again. "No, not at all. I suppose…well, you don't act like a Brewster."

"I take that as a compliment," Will said. "There were

many times growing up when I didn't feel like a Brewster. And just think—now you're one, too."

Evelyn flashed back to the moment Will had addressed her as Mrs. Brewster. How the sound of her new name—her new identity—had filled her with dread.

"I understand how it is." Evelyn could barely hear Will's voice over the sound of the violins. He continued to watch her with a bright, unconcerned expression, but his tone was serious. "It's hard work fitting into this family," he whispered. "I have no doubt you'll make a great success of it—you seem like that kind of girl—but I hope you'll think of me as a friend. Someone you can talk to if things get sticky."

"Thank you," Evelyn said. Uncomfortable with his intimate words, she glanced toward the table where Charles sat. He had his back to her, still engrossed in conversation. She saw people at the other tables watching her. Her behavior must be above reproach. She was a Brewster now.

"Will you be staying long in town?" she asked in her best society-hostess manner.

Will nodded. "I've caused enough of a stir in Europe. Time to recuperate."

"Then I'm sure I'll be seeing you at the house regularly," Evelyn said. The music was building to a climax. "I'll look forward to continuing our conversation."

"As will I," Will said smoothly. But the superficial chatter couldn't erase the bond their moment of honesty had already formed between them.

The orchestra paused before starting the next dance. Evelyn pulled her body away from Will's as he leaned over and gently kissed her hand.

"A pleasure to meet you, sister," he said. His lingering hold on her hand made Evelyn blush. Was he flirting with her at her own wedding?

Evelyn lifted the skirt of her gown and walked back to her table. She laid her hand on Charles's shoulder as she sat down and smiled when he turned to look at her. Evelyn felt she was playacting the part of a dutiful wife. Inside, her stomach was churning with excitement, her mind replaying every word of her conversation with Will.

With a sinking feeling, she wondered if she had married the wrong Brewster.

CHAPTER THREE

ALISSA COULD TELL Constance was surprised by her appearance, but she was too tired to care. She reached forward for a hug, then pulled back as she saw her friend stiffen. No wonder—Constance, as usual, was immaculate in a pressed cotton blouse and tailored trousers, while Alissa looked like a refugee from a construction site. Her greasy hair was jammed under an old college baseball cap. A paint-splattered, stretched-out T-shirt was paired with saggy pants that had a rip across one leg, and a fine layer of wood dust was sprinkled over her skin. The two women looked each other over, then broke into laughter.

"I'm so glad you're here!" Alissa exclaimed. "Ready for the tour?"

Constance clapped her hands together and pressed them to her chest, one of the prim, old-lady gestures that made her appear far older than she was. Although, at thirty-five, she was only a few years older than Alissa, Constance Powers seemed to belong to another generation. Even when her job as an architect had her traipsing through dusty building sites in a hard hat, Constance managed to stay elegant. Somewhere between a mentor and older-sister figure, Constance was the person Alissa aspired to be.

"Is this still a good time?" Constance asked. "If you're in the middle of something…"

"I'll be 'in the middle of something' for the next ten years, from the look of it," Alissa said cheerfully. "Come in—I'm ready for a break. I even made sandwiches."

Constance stepped into the middle of the foyer, then gasped as she took in the soaring staircase and chandelier hanging high above her.

"Oh, Alissa!" she exclaimed. Alissa grinned with delight. She could tell from her friend's expression that Constance saw past the paint cans and the tarps on the floor. She felt the magic of this house.

"I know it's a disaster zone," Alissa apologized. "I'm not going to invite anyone else over until I get the place in better shape."

"It's fantastic!" Constance said. "Even more so than I imagined. Give me the full tour."

Alissa guided her friend through the rooms, talking nonstop and pointing out her favorite architectural details along the way. They ended in the master bedroom, just off the landing at the top of the main staircase. Constance pulled open the French doors that opened out onto a narrow balcony above the back garden. She looked down on the white stone patio and walkway below. Bushes and weeds had long since taken over the flower beds, but the outline of the garden's elegant design was still clear.

Constance turned and walked back inside. Her eyes scanned the high-ceilinged room. A double bed, one dresser and an armchair sat forlornly in the middle of a space that could have easily held twice as much furniture. The floral-patterned wallpaper was peeling off the walls. A full-length mirror mounted in a gaudy gold frame made the room seem even larger and emptier. Constance fingered the floor-length white curtains.

"These are new, at least?" she asked.

"Yeah," Alissa said. "The old ones were so dusty, I couldn't stand it."

"Once you get this wallpaper down and put on a fresh coat of paint, it will look great," Constance said.

Alissa shrugged. "I'm concentrating on the down-stairs for now."

"At least you've got indoor plumbing," Constance joked as she peered into the en-suite bathroom. "When would you say this was done—the late fifties?"

"Whenever peach and black were considered the height of fashion." Alissa laughed.

"Well, I'm glad you're finally getting some help," Constance said. "What time did you say that guy was coming?"

Alissa glanced at her watch. A contractor recommended by Elaine, the Realtor, was due in half an hour for an interview. Alissa had hoped to hire some of the workmen she'd used in projects around Baltimore, but none were willing to drive this far.

"One o'clock," Alissa said. "C'mon—I've got lunch set up in the dining room."

The round, glass-topped dining table and silver aluminum chairs—brought from Alissa's modern condo—looked especially incongruous in the middle of the formal room. Dark wood wainscoting covered the lower half of the walls; the upper half was covered in worn burgundy velvet.

"I know it's silly to eat in this giant room when it's just the two of us," Alissa said, pushing an open bag of potato chips toward Constance. "But the kitchen is such a mess. Plus, it's so dark—it's not my favorite place to hang out."

"Ah, yes, the days before eat-in kitchens," Constance mused. "Half my jobs these days are kitchen expansions. Have you thought about knocking down that wall between the kitchen and conservatory? It would open up the whole back of the house."

"I'm not ripping out any walls," Alissa said firmly. "I want to keep the original character of the house."

"Suit yourself. You know me—always ready to tear things apart!"

"Any other changes you'd make?" Alissa asked.

"Oh, plenty," Constance teased. "But that doesn't mean the house isn't lovely as is."

"Really? You don't think I'm a complete fool for buying it?"

Constance carefully wiped her lips with her napkin, then leaned toward Alissa.

"Between you and me, I think you got the bargain of the century," she said.

Alissa laughed with relief. "Thank you. I mean—I was so sure I was doing the right thing when I signed the papers, but lately, I've wondered what I've gotten myself into."

"Of course you have. I feel like that on every job I take. There's always a hidden support beam that can't be moved or some other random complication. But this place—Alissa, it's wonderful."

Alissa grinned.

"It's got such great bones," Constance continued.

"The rooms, the way each one opens onto the other, with fantastic sight lines…it's really ahead of its time. Now, I'd open it up even more, as I said, but even just updating it will make such a difference. Didn't you say something about a bed-and-breakfast?"

"Maybe," Alissa said. "A lot of people come out here from Baltimore and Washington for the weekend. I could make extra money renting out rooms in the summer if I had to. It all depends on how my design business goes."

"And how's it going?"

"All right, I guess." Alissa shrugged. "A few of my clients from Marsh and Mason said they'd like to keep working with me. Nothing fancy—mostly basements and kids' rooms. Honestly, I've been so busy here that I don't have time to drum up new business."

"Whenever you're ready for more work, let me know," Constance said. "I've got a lot of contacts who could help get you started. Anything I can do to keep you from going back to that miserable office."

"Walking out the door was one of the greatest days of my life," Alissa agreed. "No regrets there."

"Look." Constance pursed her lips with concern. "I'm really sorry I didn't make it to your goodbye party. I wanted to be there."

"I know," Alissa said. Despite all the confidences that the two women had exchanged over the years, there was one topic Alissa didn't know how to address: Constance's desperate desire for a child. Years of trying unsuccessfully to get pregnant had finally given way to tests and doctors' visits and fertility treatments. Now, Constance and her husband, Colin, were at the mercy of a constant, ever-changing schedule of tests and procedures. When a few of Alissa's coworkers had thrown her a combination leaving-work and leaving-Baltimore party, Constance had called to say she wouldn't be there because she had a hospital appointment early the next morning. Alissa hadn't needed to ask why.

"So, the hospital?" Alissa asked carefully.

Constance shook her head slowly. "No luck. But thanks for asking. There's some good news, though," she said with a determined smile. "I met with another specialist, and he thinks I'm a good candidate for a new kind of treatment. I'll spare you the gory details—it probably won't be pleasant—but it's worth a shot."

"I'll keep my fingers crossed," Alissa promised. "If you ever want to talk about it…"

Constance nodded. "I know."

Alissa took in her friend's wistful expression and changed the subject. "So, how does Colin like his new job?" Alissa asked.

"It's good enough for now. Keeping the books for a dysfunctional family business was never his long-term ambition, but at least he'll get some decent stories out of it." Constance's husband had been laid off from a large accounting firm a year earlier, and Alissa had watched them both grow steadily more frustrated with his fruitless job hunt. Constance had even implied they would have to take a break from fertility treatments because of financial worries. But now that Colin was employed again, things seemed to be looking up.

"Have you heard from Brad?" Constance asked.

"Nope. Thank God. I don't need the distraction," Alissa lied. In reality, she was hurt that he hadn't called once, even though she'd left her new number on his voice mail. After talking every day for years, it seemed impossible that they now had nothing to say. Not that she wanted to get back together. It just felt strange to have him so absent from her life.

"His loss," Constance said. Their laughter was interrupted by a knock on the front door.

"Ah, it's your new handyman!" Constance announced. "Should I get going? I don't want to be in the way of the big interview."

"No, please stay," Alissa urged. "I'd love a second opinion."

As the two women walked toward the front door, Constance whispered, "Do you think he's still got all his teeth?"

"I don't care if he's toothless *and* bald," Alissa whispered back. "As long as he's strong enough to pick up a hammer."

Still smiling, she pulled open the heavy wood door. Her smile froze and her eyes widened in surprise. The man standing before her was far from the grizzled, feeble handyman she had envisioned. Instead, she faced a man not much older than herself, with muscular shoulders and biceps that nicely filled out his gray T-shirt. She was struck by his green eyes, which stared at her intently as if equally taken with her. He ran one hand through his longish, dark brown hair, shaking her out of her reverie.

"Alissa Franklin?" he asked.

"Daniel Pierce?"

His eyes crinkled amid laugh lines as they shook hands. "Call me Danny," he said.

"Danny." She stood unmoving, still trying to reconcile this vigorous man with the decrepit figure she had expected.

"Can I come in?" Danny asked, gesturing to the hallway behind her.

"Of course," Alissa said, embarrassed by her awkwardness. "Um, this is my friend Constance. She's just visiting. I mean, she's an architect, so she might have some questions for you, too. Just, you know, to get another perspective."

Constance stepped forward to block Alissa's nervous chatter. "Nice to meet you, Danny." She gripped his hand with both of hers, then turned her back to him and gave Alissa a wide-eyed smile. "Hot!" she mouthed.

Danny ran a hand down his face as though stifling a laugh. Mortified that he might have caught Constance's reaction, Alissa stiffened her shoulders and fixed Danny with her best professional expression.

"I'm sorry," Danny said good-naturedly. "I shouldn't be surprised. I just thought you'd be much older."

Alissa relaxed. "I thought the same thing about you."

And with that, the nervousness lifted. Alissa felt like herself again. How many times had she interviewed workmen for projects? She could do this almost without thinking. As they sat at the dining room table and Alissa described her plans for the house, she ignored Constance's meaningful looks and teasing asides. Constance—happily married for almost ten years—could enjoy a harmless flirtation. Alissa, on the other hand, would be this man's employer. She had to make it clear she wasn't angling for a date. No matter how hot he was.

Taking Danny on a walk through the house, Alissa

was struck by his silence. He didn't try to impress her, although his occasional comments showed a more than passable knowledge of architecture and design. Unlike so many other men she'd met in construction, he didn't come on strong. If anything, he appeared too thoughtful—something she had never encountered in a workman before.

"I'll need to check your references," Alissa said as they returned to the front door.

"Sure." Danny pulled a crumpled, folded piece of paper from his jeans pocket. "There are some names and numbers on here."

She took the worn sheet and unfolded it gingerly. He hadn't put much effort into the presentation. Would he be this cavalier about his work?

"Thanks," Alissa said. "I'll be in touch."

"I hope so," Danny said. "It's a great house. I've driven by it so many times, wondering if anyone would ever fix it up. If I had the money, I would've bought it myself."

Afterward, Alissa deflected Constance's teasing about the hunky handyman.

"I can't hire the first person who shows up," she protested.

But deep down, she knew she would, because he felt the same way about the house as she did. He would give it the respect it deserved. His good looks were just a bonus.

To AVOID LOOKING too eager, Alissa waited a full twenty-four hours before calling Danny and offering him the job. If he guessed that she hadn't interviewed anyone else, he didn't let on, telling her he was glad to be chosen and would be there the next morning to get started. About half an hour later, Elaine Price called.

"So, I hear you've hired Danny," she announced cheerily.

"Word travels fast," Alissa said.

"The downside of life in a small town, I'm afraid. Everyone knows everything. Danny's mother and I are old friends, and I told her to call me as soon as she heard. He's a very responsible worker—you won't be disappointed."

"Thanks for the recommendation." Elaine's words echoed the description she had gotten from Danny's references the night before. Dependable. Honest. Hardworking. No one volunteered the information she really wanted: why someone like him—handsome, smart, well-spoken—was working as a glorified carpenter in the middle of nowhere.

"I'm glad you're finally getting some help," Elaine said. "Though I'm impressed with what you've accomplished on your own."

Elaine seemed like the kind of person who'd call an electrician to help her change a lightbulb.

"There was one more thing I wanted to mention," she continued. "I was at the library yesterday—have you been there yet?"

"No," Alissa said. "I've barely left the house since I moved in, except to run to the hardware store."

"I got to talking with Claire Polley, who's been the librarian there for ages. I mentioned you and the house, and she said the library has a whole box of materials on the Brewsters. You should talk to her. That is, if you're still interested in the history of the house."

"Oh, yes," Alissa said. "Very much so."

"Good," Elaine said. "Claire works Mondays through Thursdays. On Fridays and Saturdays, the new girl's there. She's sweet but quite useless. Claire's the one you want."

"I'll try to get down there later this week," Alissa said. But as soon as she hung up the phone, she found herself distracted from her latest project, stripping paint off a doorway molding. She glanced at her watch. Three-thirty. If she hurried, she would have an hour or so to glance through the documents. There might even be pictures of the house. Maybe, if she found one of the home's interior, she could restore the rooms to their original decor. She could bring the house back to the way it used to be, when it was filled with happiness and love.

Alissa spotted Claire as soon as she entered the library. She was a delicate older woman who looked as if she had been living among the stacks for decades. Her curly white hair was almost the same shade as her pale white skin, and when she reached out to shake Alissa's hand, her arms were nearly translucent, revealing the veins beneath the surface.

"No one's looked at this for years," she said, "so it's all a bit dusty." She pointed to a document box in a corner behind her desk. "I'm not even sure what's here. The contents were never cataloged, I'm afraid."

Alissa carried the box to a long table in the center of the room. She removed the top and saw a stack of magazine and newspaper clippings piled loosely inside. She scanned the headline on the first article: Brewster Mansion Falls to the Wrecking Ball.

"I don't know much about the family," Claire said, "but I'll try to help you if I can."

Alissa nodded distractedly. Claire's voice had already faded into the background. She dug through the articles, going back from the 1960s to the 1920s, reading stories about the Brewster Shipping Company and tea parties given by women of the town. Then, toward the bottom, she spotted a headline.

Lavish Brewster Wedding Dazzles. The date on the newspaper was April 21, 1904.

Alissa read the subhead: Charles Brewster Introduces His Bride to Baltimore Society.

She pulled out the article, staring at a photo of a young couple standing together, facing the camera. Charles and Evelyn Brewster. He seemed stiff and serious; she clung to his arm, wearing a formal gown with puffed sleeves, a shy fairy-tale heroine clutching her dashing prince.

Suddenly, Alissa envied them with a force that caught her by surprise. For months, she had heard her new home described as the Brewster house. But the Brewsters themselves had remained shadowy figures. Now, finally, she would find out who they'd really been—and what had happened to them.

CHAPTER FOUR

ON HER FIRST DAY in her new home, Evelyn awoke to find her husband gone. A slight young woman was standing in the doorway. She almost dropped the tray she was holding when Evelyn sat up.

"Excuse me!" the girl said, hunching her body as if to hide behind the tray.

"It's Peggy, isn't it?" Evelyn asked. She remembered the maid's face from the night before, when she and Charles had returned from their honeymoon and been introduced to the household staff Alma had hired.

"Yes, Mrs. Brewster."

Evelyn patted the quilt next to her. "You can put that down here," she said, pointing toward the tray.

"Mrs. Gower wasn't sure what you took for breakfast and asks if you'll speak with her later. She can make anything you want. Some ladies hardly eat anything in the morning, as you know, but I said I thought you'd want a hearty meal after all your travels. Oh! I was supposed to ask if you take coffee, because I could get you that instead of tea if you prefer."

Evelyn smiled at the maid's nervous chatter.

"This smells delicious," Evelyn said, looking over the plate of eggs, toast and fresh berries. "Tea is perfect.

Is it customary for the ladies of the family to take breakfast in their rooms?"

Peggy's face crumpled with concern. "Oh dear, I don't know, Mrs. Brewster. I do what Mrs. Gower tells me. She worked in the kitchen at Mrs. Brewster's. I mean, the older Mrs. Brewster, Mrs. Brewster."

Evelyn smiled reassuringly. "Thank you, Peggy. Oh—one more thing. Is Mr. Brewster downstairs?"

"No, ma'am. He went out quite early. Six o'clock or so, I'd say."

"Thank you."

Peggy pulled the door shut behind her, and Evelyn was left to face the beginning of her new life alone.

It had been just a week since her wedding, but the days had passed in a blur of activity. Charles and Evelyn had spent their first night as man and wife at the Palace Hotel in Baltimore. As soon as they'd entered their suite, Charles had started pulling at the hooks and tiny buttons that fastened her elaborate gown.

"Good Lord!" he exclaimed. "This must be the true test of a husband!"

She joined in his laughter, and that shared moment calmed her enough to face what came next. Once her gown was discarded, Charles pushed her onto the bed and pulled her underskirts aside. She lay nervously rigid beneath him, not knowing what to expect. He thrust into her body while she held her breath, wincing and wondering how long the pressure would last. After a few minutes, Charles rolled off her.

"That's it, then," he sighed. "You should find it less painful next time." He paused and gave her a quick assessing look. "Wash up, darling, you look a fright!"

In the bathroom, she stared at her reflection in the mirror. Her face was flushed in embarrassment. Her hair hung in tangled ringlets. She turned on the tap and took a few moments to enjoy the luxury of warm water spilling over her hands and wrists. She washed up as best she could, then changed into one of the silk nightgowns her mother had sewn for her trousseau. She listened for a moment at the door when she was ready, but heard nothing. What happened now? Would Charles pounce on her again?

She opened the door slowly and peeked out. Charles lay on the bed in his underclothes, his jacket and trousers flung on the floor. He was snoring.

Evelyn tiptoed to the other side of the bed and slid under the covers, careful not to disturb him. Her body was exhausted, but her mind hummed with thoughts that kept sleep at bay.

The following day, Charles whisked her off for a week in New York. There were dinner parties every night, a visit to the opera, carriage rides through Central Park and shopping trips to expensive boutiques.

"You're a Brewster now," Charles said. "You need to look like one."

Charles insisted on socializing with his friends from Harvard and their wives. Confident and sophisticated, these young couples intimidated Evelyn into silence. She did little more than hang on to Charles's arm and look up at him adoringly when required. He was easy to admire then, with his elegant clothes and impeccable manners. The way he pulled her to his side and took her hand when he introduced her as "my wife" made her blush with pleasure.

Their only moments alone came late at night. Evelyn would retire to their hotel room first, while Charles enjoyed a cigar or a last card game downstairs. She would change into her nightgown, brush her hair smooth, then lie in bed and wait for him. When he came in, he would toss his jacket off in the darkness with the abandon of one who has always been catered to. There were no words, only his hands pulling her body close, his lips kissing her urgently. She lay stiff and quiet, unsure what he expected of her. He did what he needed while she concentrated on breathing until he was done. Overall, it wasn't as bad as she'd feared it might be. But not as life-altering as she'd hoped for, either.

Now she was home. A beautiful place where she felt like an intruder. After picking at her breakfast, she got dressed and went downstairs. She walked through the rooms aimlessly, wondering how she was supposed to fill her day.

"May I help you, ma'am?"

It was Mrs. Trimble, the housekeeper, a gloomy woman who shuffled through the foyer as if sleepwalking.

"Oh, yes," Evelyn said, summoning an air of confidence. "I'd like to discuss the household arrangements. That is, if you're not otherwise occupied."

Mrs. Trimble stared at Evelyn blankly. Clearly, there were no other demands on her time.

Evelyn began by asking Mrs. Trimble to tell her about the domestic staff. Peggy, the nervous housemaid, did the cleaning and served meals. Mrs. Gower, the cook, produced three-course lunches and dinners daily. Mrs. Trimble supervised Peggy, kept the house organized and handled all transactions with shopkeepers and tradesmen. Her husband and adolescent son tended the garden. The Trimbles lived in a small house on the edge of the property, next to the garden sheds; Peggy and Mrs. Gower had rooms on the third floor.

"Mrs. Brewster brought us on as a courtesy," Mrs. Trimble told Evelyn, "until you've hired the rest of your staff."

"Who else could I need?" Evelyn asked. Weren't six people more than enough to look after one married couple?

"You'll want a lady's maid, surely?" Mrs. Trimble asked. "Another housemaid or two. Perhaps a kitchen girl to help Mrs. Gower, once you start entertaining."

"Are newlyweds expected to entertain so soon?"

Mrs. Trimble shrugged. "You may do as you please."

This, Evelyn soon discovered, was Mrs. Trimble's response to most of her questions. After a frustrating day sitting around the house, waiting for Charles to return, Evelyn realized there was one other person she could turn to. Someone who would tell her exactly what life as Mrs. Brewster entailed. She wrote a note to Alma, inviting her for tea the next day. Just before asking Mr. Trimble to take it to the main house, she scribbled at the bottom of the page, *Will is welcome to join us.*

Later, Evelyn was grateful she had added that postscript, because the afternoon would have been excruciating without him. When Alma arrived, she greeted Evelyn at the door with a stiff handshake. Will, by contrast, embraced her with a delighted cry of "Sister!" The warmth of his welcome gave her strength for the ordeal ahead.

After they had settled in the parlor, Alma looked around and said, "You've certainly got work to do."

"The house, you mean?" Evelyn asked.

"Did no one give a thought to decor?" Alma asked, shaking her head disapprovingly.

Evelyn glanced around the vast, mostly empty parlor. There were no curtains on the windows, no rugs over the dark wood floors. The furniture had been placed haphazardly in the middle of the room.

"Mother redecorates constantly," Will said. "She believes a room is not fit to live in until every piece of furniture has been draped in fabric and every surface invaded by china figurines."

"One's house is a reflection of oneself," Alma said, ignoring him. "If a home appears neglected, one may assume the owner is as well."

"I agree," Evelyn said. "That's why I was anxious to talk to you. I need guidance on so many things. Decorating is certainly one of them. Also, which activities I might occupy myself with, while Charles is at work."

"My dear, I cannot be your nursemaid," Alma said. "I lead a very busy life. In fact, I canceled another engagement to come here today."

"I'm so sorry, I didn't realize—"

"However," Alma interrupted, "I can share a few thoughts." From her tone, it was clear she was issuing orders, not suggestions. "You'll want to start with the house. My secretary can give you a list of workmen and suppliers—the people to see about wallpaper and drapes and whatnot. They are mostly in Baltimore, but I assure you it's worth the journey. Did Charles hire a driver for you?"

Evelyn shook her head. "I don't think so. He hasn't mentioned it."

"How irresponsible of him." Alma sighed in annoyance. "I suppose you could use one of our carriages, when they are not otherwise engaged."

"Or I could take you in my motorcar," Will offered. Evelyn smiled. "I've never ridden in one."

"Then I insist," Will said. "Tell me the day."

"Don't be ridiculous," Alma scolded. "You'll do no such thing, Evelyn. It's no way for a lady to travel."

"Ladies in London and Paris travel by motorcar all the time, Mother," Will said.

"I'll arrange for a driver," Alma insisted, looking at Evelyn. She reached into her embroidered bag and pulled out a piece of paper. "This is a list of families we socialize with. I took the liberty of ordering visiting cards for you. You'll have a few weeks to settle in, but then you'll need to make calls and introduce yourself. Lavinia will host a lunch next week where you may get acquainted with the young married women in her circle. You'll be expected to hold dinner parties at least once a month, although you must coordinate with my secretary to make sure we're not entertaining the same day. And don't forget to speak with Charles's secretary at the office. He usually spends a few nights each week in the city."

"Oh, I hadn't realized," Evelyn murmured, trying to keep up with Alma's admonitions.

"I do encourage charity work," Alma continued, "but it must be an appropriate cause. We can discuss that another time. It's nearly four o'clock, and I still have errands in town. Charles did tell you I'm having you both to dinner this evening?"

"No, he didn't," Evelyn said, flustered. "Thank you, that sounds lovely. Oh—before you go, there was one other thing I wanted to ask. About Beatrice. Since she is now without a governess, and I'm not very busy at the moment, I thought we might continue our lessons."

Alma stared at her in horror.

"Only until you can find her a new governess," Evelyn offered.

"Absolutely not!" Alma exclaimed. "What a preposterous idea!"

"Seems rather convenient to me," Will said.

"It would never do," Alma said sternly. "Perhaps you do not understand your new position, Evelyn. You are Mrs. Brewster now. Soon enough, God willing, you'll have your own children to tend to."

"Of course," Evelyn said, trying to hide her disappointment. "It's only—I miss her. We used to spend so much time together."

"You may call on Lavinia whenever you please," Alma said. "She is your sister now, not your employer." She stood up and walked toward the front door. Without looking back, she called for Will to join her.

Will remained in the foyer next to Evelyn. "Mother, I'd rather walk back to the house. I have no reason to go into town."

"Very well," Alma said. "But I won't have you moping around much longer. It's time you were out, being seen."

"Yes, Mother," Will said. "A Brewster must always be seen. Otherwise, he might as well not exist."

Evelyn and Will watched from the front doorway as Alma's carriage took off down the drive.

"Thank goodness she's gone." His eyes sparkled with mischief. "Now we can have a real talk!"

Evelyn smiled in relief.

"No doubt you've heard I'm a terribly bad influence," Will said in a mock-serious tone.

Evelyn shrugged, unsure how to respond, and Will leaned toward her.

"It's all true, I'm afraid," he confided. "Come—I want to show you something." He took her by the hand and led her back through the parlor. Although she barely knew him, Evelyn felt immediately at ease with Will—just as she had at her wedding reception. With him, she could be simply Evelyn, not Mrs. Brewster.

They walked through the conservatory, a glass-walled room lined with potted palm trees and ferns. Opening a door at the far end, Will led Evelyn outside. They emerged onto a patio, facing a marble fountain. Beyond them, a wide lawn extended down a hill, framed by flower beds along either side. Gravel walkways led off to the right and left, disappearing behind evergreen hedges as tall as Evelyn.

"This way." Will pulled her along behind him, following the walkway to the right as it curved along the hedges. They passed a stone bench shaded by trees, then stepped into a field of wildflowers.

"Look over there." Will pointed across the field, toward a grove of trees in the distance.

"Oh!" Evelyn exclaimed as she spotted the gray stone walls of Alma's house in the distance.

"It only takes about five minutes to walk from here," Will said. "Not that I'd suggest traipsing through the fields before dinner. Mother would not approve."

"She most definitely would not," Evelyn agreed.

They stood together quietly for a few moments, listening to the wind rustle through the tall grass. Evelyn felt cut off from the rest of the world. From everything that made her life so complicated.

"I was wondering…" Will began, then paused.

Ask me anything, Evelyn wanted to say. Instead, she waited in silence.

"How are you settling in?" Will asked finally.

"Very well," Evelyn said. "Or—I should say, as well as could be hoped."

"Mother's a terrible snob. But you know that already. Don't let her lectures discourage you."

"There's a lot to live up to," Evelyn said. "The Brewster name and all it entails."

"The Brewsters," Will snorted. "We're lucky to have you. Charles should be grateful."

Charles. The name hovered between them like a warning sign.

"He's my brother, and I probably shouldn't be saying this," Will continued, "but he can't be an easy man to live with."

Evelyn thought back to her wedding night. Charles pinning her to the bed as she lay silently.

"Charles plans on spending much of his time in Baltimore," she said slowly. "Perhaps that will make things easier." She smiled to show she was joking, but Will looked at her seriously.

"There you have it," he said. "Charles, with a lovely young wife, is never at home. And I, a hopeless bachelor, am at home too much."

"You're hardly hopeless, from what I hear."

Will's eyes lit up with amusement. "Indeed? Have you heard tales of me breaking hearts across Europe?"

"Perhaps."

"Greatly exaggerated," he assured her. "I will admit to the broken engagement, but nothing else."

"Broken engagement?"

"I'm surprised Mother hasn't mentioned it," Will said. "She's so practiced at listing my faults. There's not much to the story, really. Mother found me a suitable girl, we were going to marry and settle on the estate— this very spot, actually. I designed this house and planned the gardens myself."

"Oh, I never realized…" Evelyn began.

"No matter," Will went on. "One morning, about a month before the wedding, I woke up barely able to breathe. The life ahead of me was so terrifying I thought I would die. I wrote a letter to the girl, left a note for Mother and rode to Baltimore that very day. By evening, I was on a boat to France. I stayed away for seven years. Enough time to forget I was a Brewster."

"What made you come back?" Evelyn asked.

"When I heard Charles was getting married," Will said, "I realized I was too old to run anymore. It's time to face my responsibilities. I was a coward to leave in the first place."

"Some would say it was very brave, starting afresh as you did."

"I did think it was brave at the time," Will admitted. "But I should note that I visited our bankers before I left. I wasn't brave enough to leave the family money behind. But I managed to support myself most of the time I was gone."

"How?"

"Painting portraits, at first. Society girls on tour and

that sort of thing. Acting as a guide and translator for Americans abroad. Racing motorcars."

"That explains your dashing arrival at my wedding!" Evelyn teased.

"If you're willing to risk life and limb, I would be happy to drive you to Baltimore," Will said. "I promise not to attempt any speed records along the way."

"Would your mother be appalled if I agreed?" Evelyn asked.

"Yes," Will said. "That's why you must do it."

Evelyn pretended to be torn. But they both knew what her answer would be.

"Tomorrow," Will said. "Let's say ten o'clock? We'll do your shopping, then I'll take you to lunch."

It didn't take Evelyn long to give in. After watching Will walk across the field, she stayed in the garden, strolling back and forth along the path, thinking over their conversation. She was still there when Peggy rushed outside, announcing in a panicky voice that Mr. Brewster was home. Evelyn suddenly remembered they were expected at Alma's for dinner, and she hurried inside.

She found Charles in the bedroom, his shirt and jacket flung on the floor, washing his face.

"Welcome home," she greeted him, leaning in to kiss his cheek.

"This is why men get married," he declared. "To be met by a pretty young wife at the end of a long day."

Evelyn blushed with surprised delight. She was quickly learning that Charles's moods were unpredictable. The evening before, distracted by work, he had barely spoken to her. She had spent a sleepless night worrying that she'd offended him somehow. If Evelyn had hoped the ring on her finger would improve her confidence, the effect had yet to take hold. She still felt like a helpless servant in Charles's presence, subject to her master's whims and inordinately pleased when he tossed a compliment her way.

"I had your mother to tea today," Evelyn said as she began sifting through the dresses in her armoire. "Good thing, too, otherwise I wouldn't have known we were expected for dinner tonight."

"I can't be expected to supervise our social calendar," Charles snapped.

Evelyn turned, her heart sinking at his change in tone.

"Mother's invitation slipped my mind completely," Charles said. "If you wish to berate me for that oversight—"

"Not at all," Evelyn interrupted. "I was simply making conversation. I meant nothing by it."

Charles stared at her, assessing her sincerity.

"Forgive me," he said smoothly. "I lived my whole life in the household of an overbearing woman, and I have no intention of repeating the experience." He stepped toward Evelyn and took her hands in his. "I ask very little in a wife. Someone who welcomes me home, sees to my comfort and makes no demands."

He said the words gently, his fingers caressing her palms, yet Evelyn felt strangely uneasy.

"You have free rein in all household matters," Charles said, "but I must remain my own man."

"Of course," Evelyn said, wondering what he meant.

"Then we understand each other." Charles bent to

kiss her forehead, but Evelyn was left feeling more lost than ever.

That night, watching Charles and Will at Alma's dinner table, Evelyn was struck by the differences between the brothers. Charles addressed Evelyn as if she were a guest at a formal dinner party, while Will spoke to her as a friend. Charles didn't ask her a single question, but Will wanted to know her impressions of New York and her plans for the house. Most disturbing to Evelyn were her own reactions to the two men. With Charles, she felt bumbling and unsophisticated. But when she turned to Will, her shoulders relaxed and she found herself smiling for no reason.

Riding home in the carriage that night, Evelyn told Charles about Will's offer to take her to town.

"At least he's making himself useful," Charles said. "God knows what he does with his days. There's more than enough work at Brewster Shipping, but he wants nothing to do with it. Other than the profits, of course!" His laugh was bitter.

"I do feel sorry for him, roaming around that house with only Alma for company," Evelyn said. "Perhaps I'll invite him for lunch from time to time."

Charles shrugged. "If you like. Perhaps you'll be a good influence on him. Actually…" His eyes lit up with inspiration. "You might take him along on some of your social calls. Show that he's back in circulation. He had a disastrous engagement some years ago, but I imagine he's been forgiven by now."

"He is a Brewster, after all." Will would have sensed the mockery in her tone, but not Charles.

"Exactly," he said. "Mothers will be knocking each

other over to secure him for their daughters. You could be his chaperone, make him look more respectable. You think you could polish him up?"

"I'll do my best," Evelyn said.

So, with her husband's blessing, Evelyn and Will became friends. Their jaunts into Baltimore became the highlight of her week. They laughed as they bounced over the country roads, and even with a massive hat and veil, Evelyn arrived in town dusty and windblown. Once, Will reached out to push her hair off her face, and she felt her cheeks warm with his touch.

"Your mother has set me a daunting challenge," Evelyn confided to him over their first lunch. "She has promised the *Chronicle* photographs of my house for their society pages."

"That rag!" Will grimaced. "Were you given no choice?"

"Apparently not," Evelyn said. "I'm to give them the grand tour as soon as possible, but I've barely started decorating. I haven't the faintest idea what to do."

"Have no fear," Will said. "I'll get everything sorted out."

And he did, revealing a fine eye for color and texture as he picked out wallpaper patterns and carpets. Over the months, Evelyn watched her house slowly transform from an empty shell into a warm, welcoming home. The day before the photographer was due, Evelyn and Will stood in the parlor, surveying their work.

"Do you think it's ready?" Evelyn asked.

"It's perfect," Will declared. "You'll dazzle them, Mrs. Brewster."

Behind them, the front door opened, and Charles

walked in. Evelyn was taken aback; he rarely came home before dark.

"What's going on here?" Charles asked in amusement. "Am I interrupting something?"

"Of course not!" Evelyn rushed over to give him a quick kiss on the cheek. "The photographer is coming tomorrow. We were just making a few last-minute adjustments."

"Ah." Charles looked around the room quickly. "Looks good enough." He turned to Will and smiled broadly. "Evelyn tells me you've been quite a help. I had no idea you had such a flair for home furnishings." The mockery in his voice made Evelyn nervous. She avoided meeting Will's eyes.

"I'm quite hurt you haven't offered to paint something for us," he continued. "We could hang one of my brother's masterpieces over the mantel, couldn't we, darling?"

"Alas, I have put my paintbrushes away for good," Will said smoothly. "Evelyn—it's time I was going. Mother will hold me responsible if supper is late."

"Oh, yes!" Charles urged. "Don't keep Mother waiting!"

Will nodded to Evelyn. She wanted to tell him how much she loved the house he'd created for her. She wanted to say that he had turned this imposing building into a home. Instead, she let Will walk away with nothing more than a quick goodbye.

"Still in thrall to Mother," Charles said, shaking his head. "You'd think it would drive him mad, living back in that house after all those years in Europe."

Until tonight, Charles hadn't seemed concerned

about the time Evelyn spent with Will. But she had seen something register in his face this evening, an acknowledgment of the intimacy she and Will had long since taken for granted. Although she had done nothing wrong, Evelyn knew she needed to move the subject away from Will.

"I'll tell Mrs. Gower you're home," Evelyn offered. "Are you hungry?"

"I had a late lunch at the club," Charles said. "We'll eat later."

Evelyn nodded. The seasons had shifted from spring through summer since her marriage to Charles. Already, scattered leaves in the garden were showing touches of brown. But Evelyn was no more comfortable with her new life. The headstrong young governess of a year ago had been replaced by a shy, unsure bride, dependent on her husband for guidance. Had Charles been a different sort of man, she might have confided her worries in him, her fears of never being able to live up to the Brewster name. But Charles despised weakness. He expected her to make his life run smoothly, not upset its balance. If only she knew how to please him.

"I'll tell Mrs. Gower to serve at eight," Evelyn said. She walked slowly down the hall toward the kitchen, preparing to face an evening with the husband who remained a stranger to her.

CHAPTER FIVE

ALISSA PUT ASIDE the newspaper announcement of Charles and Evelyn Brewster's wedding. She had stared at the photo of the couple for a long time, hoping for some insight into who they were, but their solemn faces revealed nothing. The story itself gave only a brief summary of the event: the wedding was held April 20, 1904, at the Oak Hill Episcopal Church. More than three hundred guests attended. Mr. and Mrs. Charles Brewster would be honeymooning in New York before returning to their home on Mrs. Alma Brewster's estate.

Alissa had just finished sifting through a pile of Brewster Shipping business records when she spotted something familiar. She carefully pulled out a faded newspaper article with a photo of her home's grand staircase, winding up from the foyer. The bottom of the crystal chandelier hung at the top of the frame. In the middle of the picture was a young woman, her hair pinned on the top of her head in a neat arrangement of curls, wearing a simple white blouse and dark skirt. The picture was too grainy to get a good look at her features.

Alissa read the caption.

Mrs. Charles Brewster welcomes the *Chronicle* to her new home. The former Evelyn O'Keefe is graciousness personified, and we look forward to her presence at Baltimore's most glittering affairs.

Alissa scanned the article. It was a fawning appreciation of all things Brewster, from Charles's good looks—"the most eligible bachelor in Maryland"—to his wife's modesty, recounted as "Mrs. Brewster is loath to accept credit for her good taste." There were three other pictures: the parlor, filled with overstuffed furniture and knickknacks; the dining room, with a dark wood table big enough to seat twenty; and the lovingly tended garden, with flower-filled beds and neatly trimmed hedges. The contrast to the current ramshackle state of the backyard was striking.

Alissa pulled a small notebook from her purse and wrote descriptions of the design elements she could see in the pictures. The article mostly gushed over the house without offering specific details, and Evelyn herself was only quoted a few times. Everything she said was frustratingly vague. Alissa read on.

Mrs. Brewster takes an active interest in the garden. For her, it is a place of refuge. While this new bride has yet to entertain on a grand scale, she promises that we will not be denied her hospitality in the months to come. "I have been so warmly welcomed into the family," she says. We eagerly await details of Mrs. Brewster's future endeavors, which assuredly will be a triumph.

Alissa put the article aside and looked through the rest of the box. There were a few more clippings from the same newspaper, including a short piece headlined A Grand Celebration for Charles Brewster:

A Who's Who of Baltimore society celebrated at the home of Mr. and Mrs. Charles Brewster on Saturday evening. The occasion was Mr. Brewster's birthday, and credit for the night's great success goes to his charming young wife, Evelyn. The house sparkled into the early morning hours, and our ladies have never looked lovelier. Mrs. Brewster was attired in an elegant gown by Foster of Philadelphia, a creation of lilac satin and crepe, accented with a sash of miniature lilies at the waist. Guests toasted Mr. Brewster with champagne and dined on roast beef, duck and venison. After dinner, the home's parlor was transformed into a ballroom, where the Roger Vellum Orchestra—well known in New York society circles—played to great acclaim. It was, all agreed, the most glamorous event seen here in recent memory. Mr. and Mrs. Brewster are rightly acknowledged as the young couple of the moment.

Clipped to the article was a sepia photograph on heavy cardstock, showing the celebrated Mr. and Mrs. Brewster in their finery. Charles stood perfectly straight, like a man used to being the center of attention. His dark eyes gazed steadily at the camera. Next to him, Evelyn appeared significantly less confident. One of her arms was hidden behind Charles, as if she were clinging to him for reassurance. Her dress, the same gauzy concoction described in the article, made her seem even less substantial. Unlike Charles, her eyes looked slightly off to one side as though she wasn't comfortable having her picture taken. Alissa tried to imagine what it had been like for a girl from her background to throw such a party. The pressure to succeed must have been enormous.

Still, it seemed she had impressed her guests. The last papers in the box were mostly clippings from newspaper social listings, mentions of parties the Brewsters had attended or charity events Evelyn had helped organize. The very last clipping was dated 1905, the year after the wedding. At the top of the page was an illustrated portrait of a handsome, dark-haired man whom Alissa immediately recognized as Charles Brewster. The picture was surrounded by a thick black border.

Hundreds Mourn Charles Brewster, the headline announced.

This was it. She would finally find out what had happened to him.

A solemn crowd gathered yesterday in St. Matthew's Church for the funeral of Charles Brewster. The eulogy was delivered by Senator G. Howard Flintock, a friend of the family. Sen. Flintock praised Mr. Brewster's charm and business acumen, saying the entire state of Maryland had suffered a great loss. Others paying their respects included...

Alissa skimmed the list of local dignitaries who had shown up. Clearly, this funeral had been as socially significant as any party.

Mr. Brewster's accidental death last week has devastated his family. His wife, Evelyn, who has remained in seclusion since the tragedy, carried herself with dignity during the service, but was not well enough to attend the reception held later that afternoon at the home of Mrs. Alma Brewster. Another notable absence was that of Mr. William Brewster, Charles Brewster's older brother, who was traveling at the time of the accident and could not be reached.

Alissa had seen this mysterious William mentioned only once before, in the list of guests at Charles and Evelyn's big party. It seemed strange they couldn't track him down for something as important as his brother's funeral. Then again, those were different times. No cell phones, no twenty-four-hour cable news. If someone decided to travel without a fixed itinerary, they'd be unreachable. Alissa tried to imagine what it must have been like for him to come home and find his brother dead. She thought about Evelyn, grief-stricken, living alone in the house. What had happened to her?

Alissa surveyed the stacks of paper on the table in front of her. For an hour, she'd been caught up in the life of the

Brewsters. But she still didn't know how Charles had died. The newspaper had referred to an accident, but that could mean anything—a fall from a horse, a hunting trip gone wrong.

Alissa turned to the photograph she had set aside. Charles and Evelyn all dressed up for his birthday party, looking forward to a long, happy life together. They had no idea their world would be shattered less than a year later.

Carefully picking up the photo and a few clippings, Alissa stood up and walked to the library counter.

"Could I make some copies?" she asked Claire.

The elderly librarian looked at her warily. "Ten cents each," she said, as if Alissa couldn't be trusted to come up with such a vast sum.

"That's fine," Alissa said. "Also—do you have a scanner?"

Claire pursed her lips and waved her toward a back desk. "I think that's what that is. But you'll have to talk to someone else about using it. I don't have the faintest idea how, and I don't care to learn."

Alissa walked around the librarian's desk and saw a familiar flat black shape. "I've got that same model in my office," she said. After some cajoling and a donation to the Library Restoration Fund, she scanned the party photo and e-mailed herself the file. She would contact a company that created custom artwork for some of her clients and commission them to make a full-size repro-duction. She could already picture it hanging in her foyer. It would be the Brewsters' homecoming. Maybe, somehow, their presence would bring happiness back to the house.

During the five-minute walk home, Alissa waved to the few neighbors she passed along the way. In Baltimore she had kept to herself, barely speaking to the people who lived on the same floor of her condo building. Here in Oak Hill, thanks to Elaine, she already knew the names and stories of everyone within a two-block radius. As she started up her driveway, she was surprised to see an unfamiliar truck parked in front of the house. She might be on friendly terms with a number of people in town, but she didn't think any of them would show up unannounced.

"Hello?" she called out.

As she got closer, she saw that the man standing on the porch, turning toward her, was Danny.

"Hey there!" he said. "No wonder you didn't hear me knocking."

"I was at the library," Alissa said. "Can I help you with something?" They'd agreed he would start the next morning. What was he doing here?

"Yeah," he said. "You didn't say what the first project would be, so I wasn't sure which tools to bring. I was driving by here anyway, so I decided to stop by and check."

His earnestness made Alissa relax a bit. "The kitchen is my top priority for now."

"Great," Danny said. "I'll prepare myself for demolition work."

"I drew up some plans," Alissa said. "I figured we'd go over them together."

Danny nodded. "Sounds good."

"Okay, then, I'll see you tomorrow at nine."

"See you then," Danny agreed. "By the way—did you find what you needed?"

Alissa looked at him, puzzled.

"The library," he explained. "It doesn't have much of a collection. I usually go to the one in Carlsville."

"Actually, I was doing some research on the couple that built this house," Alissa said.

"Really?" The way he asked, his eyes widening with curiosity, reignited Alissa's excitement about her discoveries.

"Want to know what I found out?"

He did. Alissa sat down on the front steps, with Danny beside her. Reaching into her shoulder bag, she pulled out the photocopied articles.

"These show what the house looked like right after it was built," she began. "Here's the living room, or I guess I should say parlor. Just look at those wonderful rugs. Kind of overcrowded with furniture, though, don't you think? This room in the back—I've been calling it the greenhouse, because it had all these dead plants inside, but they called it the conservatory. You can see it a little bit here in the background. And check out the garden! Isn't it beautiful?"

Danny watched Alissa's wavy brown hair bob against her neck as she turned back and forth, pointing to the pictures and then passing the pages to him. He'd been wary of taking on a designer as a client, concerned she'd second-guess every decision he made. But listening to Alissa's voice rise with excitement, Danny found himself caught up in her enthusiasm. He flipped back to the picture of the parlor.

Alissa stopped as Danny began to laugh.

"I'm sorry," he said. "I'm not making fun of you. It's rare to find a client so enthusiastic." He took one of the pages and examined the picture of the parlor.

"There's a definite Arts and Crafts influence," he said. "You can see it in these chairs. The wallpaper looks like it could be William Morris."

"You think so?" Alissa asked.

"A family this rich could afford to import it themselves," Danny said. "I wouldn't be surprised if some of this furniture was European, too."

"Have you got some designer credentials I don't know about?" Alissa asked.

Danny shook his head. "No, I was an art history major," he said.

"Really?"

Danny nodded. "Yeah, at Boston College. Fascinating, but completely useless from a career perspective."

"I was an art major at the University of Virginia," Alissa said. "An equally useless degree."

"UVA's great," said Danny. "It was one of my top choices for grad school."

"More art history?" Alissa asked.

Danny shook his head. "An MBA at Georgetown. But that's part of my old life. I've moved on."

Moved on to what? Alissa wanted to ask. Why bother getting such an expensive, prestigious degree if all he was going to do was fix other people's houses? His determination to change the subject only made Alissa more curious.

"Getting back to the house," Danny said, "I think you're on the right track. Update where you have to but keep the original style intact."

Alissa nodded, but before she could steer the conversation back to Danny's career, he pulled out another sheet of paper and asked, "Who are they?" Alissa looked at the copy she had made of the Brewsters' wedding picture.

"These are the original owners, Charles and Evelyn," Alissa said.

"She looks scared," Danny said.

"You think so?"

Alissa leaned over Danny's shoulder. For a moment, she was distracted by the feel of his arm against hers. Then she quickly pulled away, wondering if she had lingered just a moment too long.

"I mean—she must've been nervous," Alissa said. "She was young, she didn't have any money and she was marrying into a wealthy family. This isn't a very good picture, anyway. I found a much better one of them, all dressed up for a party. I'm going to order a copy to hang in the foyer, or maybe over the fireplace. You know, welcome them back to the house...." She saw Danny smile and her voice trailed off.

"I get it," Danny said. "I'm all for appreciating a building's history. But don't let yourself get obsessed by it."

"Obsessed?" Alissa protested.

"The past can be a trap," Danny said. "It's possible to spend so much time looking backward that you never move forward." Softening his tone, he added, "That's just my opinion."

Danny handed the papers back to Alissa and stood up.

"Look," he said, "I understand why you're curious

about the Brewsters. Maybe there's some way I can help you find out more. My mom knows every gossipy old lady in the county."

Eager to show there were no hard feelings, Alissa agreed. "That would be great."

"I'd better get going," he said.

As he walked away, Alissa slid the photocopies into her bag and turned toward the front door. She was surprised how much Danny's criticism had stung her. Already, it seemed, she valued his opinion. But maybe his lecture about the past had more to do with him than her. She tried to imagine Danny—with his stained jeans and ratty T-shirts—sitting in a management class. Had he flunked out and been too embarrassed to say so? Or had he gotten a job and made a mess of it, something humiliating enough to drive him out of the business world?

She wanted Danny's respect, the same respect she expected from anyone who worked for her. If forced to be completely honest with herself, she would even admit to the first faint stirrings of a crush. But no matter how good-looking Danny was, Alissa wouldn't completely trust him until she found out more about the man he used to be.

CHAPTER SIX

EVELYN HAD NEVER planned a seduction. Imagining what might be required made her so nervous that she never would have followed through if she hadn't been desperate. It was six months since the wedding, and Charles hadn't softened into a loving husband. If anything, he treated Evelyn more formally than ever. Intimate relations were less frequent—once a week, at most—and ended without a word. Charles either fell asleep immediately afterward or left for his study to continue working. Most mornings, she woke up alone.

Evelyn tried to confide in her mother, but Katherine was willfully oblivious. She only wanted to talk about Evelyn's beautiful house and the parties she attended. For Katherine, her daughter's life sparkled with possibility and Evelyn couldn't bring herself to disillusion her. If she hadn't longed for something else, she might have been content. She could have been one of the many women she'd met who tolerated rather than loved their husbands. But that was no longer enough. She had fallen in love with Will.

She had admitted the truth to herself only recently. The more time Evelyn spent with him, the more she longed for him. His humor cut through the stuffiness of local dinner parties and she often had to press a napkin to her face to hide her laughter. During their lunches together in Baltimore, he spoke to her honestly, admitting his uncertainty about the future. If Evelyn had initially been attracted to Will's exuberance, it was these quieter conversations that won her heart. She could find a cad charming, but this man who bared his soul to her was no cad. Quite the opposite.

Chatting pleasantly over Sunday dinners at Alma's, they could have been any brother- and sister-in-law enjoying each other's company. But secretly, Evelyn's feelings had intensified from friendship to desire. When Will pressed his lips against her hand as he said goodbye, she imagined herself kissing him back. With Will, she wasn't nervous young Mrs. Brewster. She was Evelyn O'Keefe again, a confident woman who wasn't afraid to speak her mind.

Evelyn felt as though she were staring over the edge of a cliff. Unspoken signals flashed between her and Will when they were alone, pauses in the conversation when each waited for the other to acknowledge what was happening. In such moments, she longed for him to say he loved her. And she hoped just as desperately that he wouldn't, because she wasn't sure she'd have the strength to turn him away.

Evelyn also knew Alma—ever vigilant of the family's reputation—couldn't possibly have missed the sparks. Sure enough, after dinner one Sunday, Alma drew her aside as they walked to the drawing room. Peering at Evelyn's midsection, she asked, "Any news?"

Evelyn stared at her in disbelief.

"A grandchild?" Alma whispered, clearly annoyed by Evelyn's reticence. Evelyn shook her head.

"I would have expected something after this long."

Evelyn couldn't look directly at Alma. She glanced around to make sure they wouldn't be overheard. Charles stood in front of the fireplace on the other side of the room, lecturing Winslow and Will. Lavinia was neatening one of her daughter's braids as Beatrice struggled to escape.

"Perhaps," Alma said coolly, "if you favored your husband with the attention you give others so readily."

"I wish for a child as much as you do," Evelyn protested.

"You must do more than wish, my dear," Alma said. "The fate of the family rests on your shoulders now. It's a heavy responsibility and one I sympathize with." Alma's eyes looked past Evelyn toward Charles, and her tone softened. "Once you have children, everything becomes more secure."

For a moment, Evelyn pictured Alma as a young bride, as bewildered by the Brewsters as Evelyn was now. Had Alma also felt crushed by the weight of family expectations?

If she had, there was no trace of it now. Alma nudged Evelyn toward Charles, giving her a meaningful look. The message was unmistakable. Evelyn must lure Charles into producing an heir.

That night, Charles ignored Evelyn's timid hints and fell asleep without touching her. As Evelyn lay in bed, reliving a moment earlier that evening when Will's hand had brushed hers, she realized the foolishness of her fantasies. She must put aside her daydreams and do whatever necessary to recapture her husband's interest. Once they had a child, her life would have purpose, and Will would fade into the background. She had first attracted Charles by challenging him. Perhaps she could do so again.

The next morning she awoke alone and determined to seduce her husband. She spent the afternoon tending to herself in a way she never had before: soaking in a hot bath, spraying on the French perfume Lavinia had given her as a wedding present, allowing her hair to fall over her shoulders. When Charles strode through the front door, she was there to greet him with a kiss.

"What's that smell?" he asked.

"It's called *Air de Joie*. A gift from your sister."

"Rather cloying," Charles said. "More suited to a French courtesan than Lavinia."

Evelyn was taken aback, but she smiled and said lightly, "And what do you know of French courtesans?"

Charles wrapped one arm around her waist. "Trying to catch me out, are you?" A flash of attraction ignited between them. Perhaps there was hope after all.

Throughout dinner, Evelyn did her best to charm him. She treated Charles like a fascinating dinner-party guest, leaning toward him and smiling encouragingly. Charles relaxed in the warmth of her admiration. Once, he even reached across the table to stroke her hair.

"You should wear it down more often," he said. "But only for me." His fingers moved down along the curve of her cheek.

"No coffee this evening," she told Peggy as the maid came in to clear the plates.

"Yes, Mrs. Brewster." Peggy offered an awkward

curtsy before leaving the room. No matter how many times Evelyn told her it wasn't necessary, Peggy insisted on treating her employers as if they were royalty.

"Are we retiring for the night already?" Charles asked.

"I thought we might find something to occupy us upstairs," Evelyn said, lowering her eyes modestly.

"Are you trying to have your way with me, wife?"

Evelyn couldn't tell if Charles was flirting or making fun of her. Perhaps both.

"Tell me," he continued, lowering his voice almost to a purr. "What do you have planned?"

Too embarrassed to say the words, Evelyn sat silently, waiting for Charles to take the lead, as he always did.

Charles smiled with a mixture of amusement and cruelty. "How disappointing. I had hoped to hear something scandalous. Or are you playing the woman of mystery?"

"Is it such a mystery why a wife would wish to have relations with her husband?" Evelyn asked.

"Don't fret, Mrs. Brewster," he said, chucking her under the chin as if she were a child. "I will do my duty. I suppose Mother has been hounding you for a grandson?"

Again Evelyn said nothing, but she knew the expression on her face confirmed his suspicions.

"I applaud your effort," Charles said. "However, let's not make a habit of such behavior, shall we? In any marriage, a husband must guide his wife, not the other way around. In fact, it can be quite unmanning for a husband to be at the beck and call of his wife's urges."

"It was not meant as an insult," Evelyn murmured.

"Then I forgive you," Charles said. "In any case, I have plans this evening with Jack Beltrain. A gentlemen's card party, which I expect will go quite late. I may even stay the night, so don't bother waiting up. Now, go wash yourself off," he ordered. "The reek of that perfume will infect the whole house."

He brushed past her, gathered his hat and coat from the hallway and slammed the front door behind him. Evelyn sat at the table until he was gone, then made her way slowly up the stairs. She went first to her bathroom, where she splashed water over her face again and again, allowing the cold to numb her. Then she dried off and stared at her face in the mirror. Her skin was pale, and her eyes were bloodshot with unshed tears.

Desperate for fresh air, she threw open the French doors in the bedroom and stepped out onto the balcony. It was already dark, a sign that winter was on its way. She looked toward the main house and saw lights glimmering faintly in the distance. She wondered if Will and Alma were still at supper. Alma was probably lecturing him, as she so often did. Evelyn pictured Will's face at once amused and annoyed. She could imagine him turning to her and rolling his eyes, if she were there, next to him.

As Evelyn stared into the darkness, toward the faraway house, a movement in the field at the edge of the garden caught her eye. As if her thoughts had called him to her, Will appeared, walking through the tall grass. She lifted her hand in greeting, and he quickened his pace. She watched him disappear between the hedges bordering the garden and waited until he emerged onto the patio below her.

"You look like Juliet," Will said, "calling to Romeo from her balcony."

She couldn't help but smile. Then, remembering Peggy and Mrs. Gower washing up in the kitchen not far away, she put a finger to her lips. "Hush," she whispered. "I'll come down."

She went back into the bedroom and pulled a shawl over her shoulders. Tiptoeing along the hallway, she went quietly down the stairs. She could hear the faint echo of voices from the kitchen and was very careful not to make a sound as she crossed the parlor and conservatory. She carefully pushed open the back door and stepped out onto the patio. Will stood against a tree, the shadows hiding him from the kitchen windows.

"Come," he whispered, holding out his hand. Evelyn followed him along the gravel walkway through an opening in the hedges, into a secluded garden room, where a stone bench sat under a maple tree. He wrapped one arm around her shoulders and pulled her down next to him on the bench. She expected him to release her once she was seated, but his arm remained, balanced lightly where it was.

He waited, as if by taking hold of her he had gone as far as he could. The rest was up to Evelyn.

"What were you doing out there in the field?" she asked.

"I had to escape," Will said. "Mother was unbearable tonight."

Evelyn remembered her mother-in-law's urging to have a child. She knew only too well the agonizing pressure of Alma's disapproval.

"I don't envy you, living with her," she said. Leaning in toward him would be so easy. Just a few inches and she would be in his embrace. But those few inches would change her life.

"And you?" Will asked quietly. "What brought you out to the balcony?"

There were so many things she could have said. Ways she could have politely deflected the conversation. But sitting next to Will, in the intimate silence of the garden, she could only speak the truth.

"Charles has been lacking in his attentions." Evelyn looked down so she wouldn't have to meet Will's eyes as she revealed her humiliation. "That is to say, his marital duties."

Will said nothing.

"I can't help but wonder—oh, it's silly, really. You'll think me such a fool."

"I promise I won't," Will said.

"It makes me wonder if he's been unfaithful." She turned to face him now. Will didn't look shocked. Only sad.

The unspoken confirmation brought the full power of Charles's betrayal crashing down. Evelyn clenched her eyes shut as her body shook with suppressed sobs.

"I'm sorry," she stammered, wiping her face with the edge of her shawl. The words tumbled out. "I shouldn't be telling you this, but marriage isn't what I imagined. I've tried so hard to be a good wife. Tonight, I did my best to make him happy, but it wasn't enough. He mocked me and left, and I faced another night alone, and I came outside, because of you. I know it's ridiculous, but looking at your house and thinking of you comforted me."

It was done. She'd told the truth. If Will chose, he could make excuses for his brother, offer the conventional reassurances. He could extricate himself with a minimum of embarrassment.

Instead, Will turned toward her and took her hands in his.

"You asked before why I was walking in the fields," he said. "The truth is that I wanted to be closer to you."

Evelyn's body tingled as she grasped the meaning of his words.

"I was torturing myself, to be honest," he continued. "I watched the lights come on in your window, and I imagined what Charles might be doing to you. My brother, who doesn't deserve you. I had resolved to turn back when you came outside. Even from that distance, I could see you were upset. I had to make sure you were all right."

Evelyn couldn't move. She sat completely still, rigid as the stone bench, as Will moved his hands to her face. He kissed her, softly, gently, sending a burst of warmth through her body.

The only other man who had ever kissed her was Charles, with a force she'd mistaken for passion. Now, as Will's lips caressed her face, she felt as if she were floating, her senses both soothed and heightened. She returned his kiss, wrapping her arms around his body. His back and shoulders were solid, something she could cling to to keep from going under. Here, in his arms, she could escape.

Suddenly, she stopped. This was madness, not escape. Kissing Will made her no better than Charles. In fact, she was worse, because everyone knew a husband was allowed to be discreetly unfaithful, but adultery in a wife was unforgivable. If she distanced herself from Will now, before things went too far, they could still remain friends. She needed his friendship more than anything else.

"I'm sorry," Evelyn stammered, releasing Will and tucking her arms tightly inside her shawl. "I don't want you to think—"

"Not at all," Will said, his tone colder, suddenly formal. "Please, no apologies. I took advantage of your distress. I am a cad, madam, as you have no doubt been told. I beg a thousand pardons."

His exaggerated formality made her laugh in spite of her embarrassment. She looked at him and was relieved to see him smile back at her.

"If things had been different," Evelyn said wistfully. "If we'd met under other circumstances…"

"I wish I had returned from Europe sooner," he said, suddenly serious. "I wish I'd met you before Charles did."

Evelyn nodded. "So do I."

"Well, then, we've had our bout of self-pity," Will said, shaking his head as if to rouse himself from a dream. "Your position is far more precarious than mine. I'm sorry if I've made things difficult for you."

"It was as much my fault as yours," Evelyn said. She longed to touch him again, but she kept her hands in her lap.

"I hope you'll still think of me as someone with your best interests at heart," Will said. "Someone who cares for you."

"Yes," Evelyn said. "As I care for you."

"I know." They looked at each other silently, acknowledging all that could have been between them.

"I should go," Evelyn said finally, rising from the bench. If she continued to sit beside him, she might do something she'd regret.

Will stood beside her. "One thing…" He paused, considering his words carefully.

"My brother has a temper," he continued. "Should you ever run into trouble, I hope you'll confide in me. We may not have opportunities to talk alone, like this, but if there's something you need to tell me, leave a note. Here, under the bench. I can come by at night without being seen."

"So it appears," Evelyn said with a smile.

Will touched her cheek lightly. "I do worry about you."

"It will all work out," Evelyn said, trying to feign a confidence she didn't feel. Will reached out and embraced her one last time, then turned and walked away. Even though she ached to run after him, Evelyn held firm. The next time she saw him, they would be surrounded by family at Alma's Sunday dinner. She would be seated next to her husband, a proper wife in her proper place. Will would simply be her brother-in-law. But now, as she wandered back to her room and changed into her nightclothes, all she could imagine was walking up the stairs, into her bedroom, with Will. She lay alone in bed chasing sleep, remembering the feel of his kisses. Tomorrow, she vowed, she would shut the door on those memories forever.

BUT THE FEELINGS that had been stirred up couldn't be tamed so easily. The next Sunday, dinner at Alma's was more difficult than ever. Charles sat next to her, barely acknowledging her presence. Across the table was Will, making his usual joking remarks. Evelyn struggled to match his light tone. She looked at his hands and remembered the feel of them on her face. She wanted to reach across the table and pull him away, out of the house, toward his motorcar. They could drive off together and disappear.

"Evelyn?"

She turned toward Alma, belatedly aware that her mother-in-law had asked her a question.

"I asked if you were feeling well?" Alma repeated.

"Yes, Mother," Evelyn said. "A bit tired, I suppose."

Alma continued to look at her appraisingly throughout dinner. After the meal, Alma pulled Lavinia aside. The two women huddled together, glancing at Evelyn from time to time. Evelyn made a point of ignoring Will as the family gathered for coffee in the parlor. She sat next to Charles and tried to appear interested as he ranted to Winslow about railroad company corruption. Will read stories to Beatrice on the other side of the room.

"I do hope we'll see you at our meeting tomorrow," Lavinia said to Evelyn as she and Charles prepared to leave.

"Of course," Evelyn said. She thanked Alma and gave Beatrice a kiss, but avoided Will on her way out. What could she possibly say to him?

Evelyn had originally had high hopes when Lavinia invited her to join her literature club, but the meeting the next day was as disappointing as ever. Evelyn had assumed the monthly gatherings would foster the sort of lively discussions she'd enjoyed in college. Instead, she found that the club members—all young married women—discussed books for no more than ten minutes, before spending the rest of the morning trading gossip. Evelyn had spent an excruciating length of time pretending to be interested in one woman's complaints about her maid when she heard Lavinia call out something about Will.

"Pardon me?" Evelyn asked.

"Is Will still driving you to town in that ghastly motorcar?"

"Occasionally," Evelyn said. "He's been very helpful with the house."

"Really?" Lavinia asked with overacted surprise. "I'd be careful, if I were you."

Why would Lavinia be warning her about Will? Panicked, Evelyn wondered what her sister-in-law knew.

"Careful?" Evelyn asked, trying to keep her voice steady.

"Those cars can be dangerous. Mr. Hadley, Emily's father, broke his leg riding in one just the other day. Honestly, I don't know why Will insists on traveling that way. It makes him look..." She paused and pursed her lips. "Disreputable."

"Really?" Evelyn asked. "I've found him nothing but respectful." She remembered the warmth of his hand against her cheek. The feel of his lips on hers.

"Oh, Evelyn." Lavinia breathed an exaggerated sigh. All other conversations in the room had trailed off, and she basked in the rapt attention of her guests. "I meant no offense. I am only offering friendly advice. I've known Will far longer than you, and he's always been a bit of a rogue. As Charles's wife, your behavior must be above reproach."

It could have been Alma speaking. Lavinia stared at Evelyn disapprovingly, her dour expression making her look far older than her years. Had Lavinia ever been young? Evelyn wondered. Laughed uproariously for no reason? Or had she been molded from birth into a miniature version of Alma, joylessly protecting the Brewster legacy?

"I assure you, I am very aware of what it means to be a Brewster," Evelyn said. The other women looked at Evelyn and Lavinia with wide eyes; this discussion would be recounted over dinner tables throughout the county tonight.

"Good," Lavinia said. "I hope we can both prevail on Will to mend his ways."

Lavinia couldn't know what had happened in the garden. But her gaze made Evelyn uneasy. Lavinia suspected something. Which meant that Alma did, too.

CHAPTER SEVEN

ALISSA TRACED her fingers along the edge of the stone bench. For decades, this pitted surface had weathered the seasons, protected only by the branches of the maple tree that curved overhead. The hedges enclosing this section of the garden had long since outgrown their beds, and the grass had been taken over by weeds. Cut off from the rest of the backyard, the space felt neglected and lonely. Alissa wondered if Evelyn Brewster had ever sat here.

She heard Danny call her name from the main yard.

"In here!" she shouted.

Danny pushed aside the unruly hedges and poked his head through.

"Come on in," Alissa said, tilting her head toward the other side of the bench.

Danny walked over and settled down next to her. Over the past few weeks, they'd fallen into a comfortable routine. Every morning, they would discuss plans for the day over coffee in the dining room. Then they got to work. Lately, Danny had been ripping out cabinets in the kitchen, while Alissa focused on her bedroom upstairs. They would meet for lunch—often sitting out on the front porch—before continuing to work late into the afternoon. Around five o'clock, they would check in and review their progress.

Today, Alissa had been stripping wallpaper in her bathroom, exhausting labor that made her shoulders and arms ache. Even with an electric fan going full blast, the sweltering summer heat made the job especially miserable. She quit work early, eager to spend a few minutes outside before the sun disappeared over the horizon. She'd wandered into this overlooked section of the garden, and decided to rest on the bench. She must have been daydreaming for quite a while, if Danny was already finished with work. Watching him sit down next to her, she found it comforting to know that someone missed her when she wandered off. Even if that person was being paid to check on her.

"Landscaping is my last priority right now," Alissa said, "but what would you think about opening all this up?"

"Here?" Danny asked.

"Yeah. Tear out the bushes, and get rid of this old bench. It would make the backyard look much bigger."

Danny looked around. "Maybe. But I kind of like it the way it is."

"Really?" Alissa was still skeptical.

"Granted, it needs work," he conceded. "The bushes should be cut way back, and it would look better with some plants around the perimeter. But I like the concept—a garden within a garden."

Alissa shrugged.

"It's a place to escape to," Danny said. "Don't you ever need that?"

"Sure," Alissa said.

But she didn't, not really. She'd never felt so removed from the rush of ordinary life. She'd quit her job and moved from the city, leaving her boyfriend and most of her friends behind. Working on the house, she spent most of her time alone. She'd found this secluded space melancholy a few minutes before, but now, with Danny sitting next to her, she reconsidered the hidden patch of green. It created a peaceful sanctuary around them, a place where they could go beyond their roles of boss and employee. For a moment, she imagined sitting with Danny on a date, his hand brushing hers as they reached for the menus in a restaurant. The way he would push his hair off his face before looking at her. How she would blush when their eyes met in the candlelight. Alissa looked at Danny's hand on the bench beside her and fought the sudden urge to touch him.

"I wanted to tell you something," Danny said.

"Yes?" Alissa asked quickly. Could he be thinking the same thing?

"It's about the original owners, the Brewsters," he said. Alissa smiled encouragingly to cover her disappointment.

"I know I made fun of you for being obsessed," Danny continued. "But I ran into someone who might be able to help. When I went to the hardware store after lunch, I saw an old friend of my mother's, Julia Larkin. She was really interested when I told her I was working over here. She's lived in town her entire life and knows everyone. Probably knows where all the bodies are buried, too. She met some of the Brewsters way back when, and says you're welcome to call her if you want to talk."

He reached into his pocket and pulled out a piece of paper with a telephone number written in shaky black ink. If this was Julia Larkin's handwriting, she must be ancient.

Alissa took the paper. "Thanks," she said. "I wonder if she knows how Charles died."

Danny cocked an eyebrow. "A hundred-year-old mystery, and you're going to solve it?"

"I need to understand what happened," Alissa explained. "I know it sounds crazy, but I feel a connection to them. They were happy here once. I owe it to them to bring that happiness back."

"You already have," Danny said.

Alissa glanced at him, but his face was turned away, looking up at the maple leaves above them. This was the closest he'd come to revealing any feelings for her. She could ask him what he meant. Find out if he thought of her as more than the person who signed his paychecks.

Or she could let the moment pass. Continue living a life without complications.

A breeze rustled through the leaves, and Alissa closed her eyes and lifted her face to it, welcoming the brief respite from the heat. When she looked up again, Danny was standing.

"I'd better clean up my stuff," he said. "You don't pay me to sit around, right?"

"It's fine…" Alissa began.

"Just making sure you get your money's worth. See you tomorrow."

The sudden change of tone threw Alissa off balance. One minute Danny was talking to her as a friend, the next he was acting like an obsequious servant. She'd worked alongside him long enough to know that he wasn't a man who had trouble taking directions from a woman. They had a comfortable, friendly rapport. But he seemed unwilling—or unable—to go beyond that. To him, she would always be the boss.

And wasn't that as it should be? Alissa stood and stretched her sore arms. Already, the spell that had settled over her in that hidden garden had been broken. Maybe it had been no more than wishful thinking.

THAT EVENING, Alissa dialed Julia Larkin's phone number.

"Oh, yes!" Julia exclaimed when Alissa introduced herself. "Danny told me all about you!" Her voice quavered, but her enthusiasm had not weakened with age.

"As he might have mentioned, I'm very interested in the original owners, Charles and Evelyn Brewster."

"Can't say I knew them personally." Julia laughed. "I'm not quite that ancient!"

"Oh, I didn't mean…" Alissa stammered.

"A joke, a joke," Julia reassured her. "We old ladies do have a sense of humor, you know. I'm thrilled someone your age is interested in local history. What do you want to know?"

"Well, anything, really. I did some research and learned that they moved into the house shortly after they were married, and that Charles died a year later. But I couldn't find out how he died."

"That's easy," said Julia. "It was an accident. A fall."

"Do you know what happened?" Alissa asked.

"It was before I was born, so I don't have all the details," Julia said. "But I remember something my mother used to say. Whenever my brother ran down the stairs too quickly, my mother would scold him and say he could die that way, it had happened to Charles Brewster, and he could be next. She was always telling stories about people dying horribly to scare us into behaving. Not that it had much effect on my brother."

Alissa pictured a body falling from the second-floor landing, tumbling over the railing to the foyer below. It was the only place in the house where a fall could have been fatal. Had Evelyn been there? Had she watched her husband die?

"It shattered the family," Julia continued. "They were never the same afterward, my mother said. Charles's mother had been a formidable woman, but she became a recluse after his death. He ran the business, you see, so when he died, their company faltered, too. By the Depression, there wasn't much left of the Brewster fortune."

"Do you know what happened to Evelyn, his wife?"

"I have no idea," Julia said. "I believe she moved away. Certainly, I never heard anything about her growing up. I wouldn't blame her for leaving and starting over somewhere else, would you?"

"No," said Alissa. Sometimes running away was the bravest choice. She knew that firsthand. "Do any Brewsters still live in the area? I know Charles had a brother and sister."

"I don't know much about the brother," said Julia. "He was something of a black sheep. As far as I know, he disappeared off to Europe or somewhere and wasn't in contact with the rest of the family. As for the sister, Lavinia, she lived here all her life. After her mother died, she moved into what we called the Brewster mansion."

"The one that was torn down?" Alissa asked.

"Yes—it was quite a place. Very elegant, but also rather intimidating. It had towering stone walls, rather like a fortress. Lavinia had only the one daughter, Beatrice. Imagine, a family of three living in that huge house! My family was invited to their Christmas party once, sometime in the early thirties. You never saw such decorations. It was one of the highlights of my childhood."

"What happened to Beatrice?" Alissa asked.

"Beatrice was a full generation older than me, so our paths rarely crossed," Julia said. "She married and moved into your house. By the time the war came along, her parents had sold the mansion, and it was being run as a school."

"So, Beatrice was the last of the Brewsters?"

"I suppose so," said Julia. "But of course her last name was Preston. I've forgotten her married name. She moved away during the war—something to do with her husband's job—and I'm not sure what happened to her. There haven't been any Brewsters here for years."

"Oh." Alissa couldn't hide her disappointment. Julia Larkin had lived in Oak Hill her whole life, but she didn't have the answers. Maybe no one did.

"There's one more person you could try," Julia said. "But he may lead you on a wild-goose chase. His name's Roger Blake. He lives outside Winchester, about ten miles from here. Calls himself a writer, but he's a troublemaker as much as anything else. For years, he's been working on a book about local unsolved crimes. He thinks it will be a bestseller, but it sounds more like an excuse to dig up old gossip. In any case, he called me a few months ago asking about the Brewsters. Claimed he'd found information about them in some archive in Baltimore. How there was more to Charles's death than met the eye, and that sort of nonsense. I thought he was talking the story up to draw attention to himself yet again, and I told him what I've told you, which isn't much. But if you think it would help, you could call him."

Alissa scribbled down the phone number Julia recited.

"Don't get your hopes up," Julia warned. "Roger is a big talker. He could be seeing something that's not really there. He prefers the tarnish to the shine."

"What do you mean?"

"He'd rather look at the dark side. I prefer an inspiring legend to the messy truth. Everyone here still talks about Charles and Evelyn Brewster because we're drawn to romantic love stories. The fact that he died young makes it all the more poignant. Does *how* he died really matter?"

Maybe not. But she couldn't give up now. Alissa had always been someone who read the end of books first. She wouldn't be able to stop until she found the ending to this story.

CHAPTER EIGHT

THERE WAS NO other choice: Evelyn would have to ask Alma for help. Whatever her mother-in-law knew or suspected about Evelyn's feelings for Will, she wanted Charles's marriage to succeed. The future of the Brewster family depended on it. If Evelyn was to produce an heir, Charles couldn't continue to leave her alone, night after night. Alma was the only person with the power to make him change.

Evelyn knew that appealing to Alma would mean humbling herself before the person who would most enjoy her humiliation. Alma had been against the marriage from the start and now, she would have even more reason to gloat. Evelyn would have to accept fault and nod at her criticisms. But the shame would be worth it if it saved her marriage. If Alma could convince Charles to treat Evelyn as his wife, rather than an irritating houseguest.

Evelyn sent a note asking if they could meet to discuss a family matter. Alma's reply arrived a few hours later, one sentence on a thick monogrammed card: "I would be happy to receive you at three o'clock tomorrow afternoon."

The next day, Evelyn started up the front steps of

Alma's house precisely at three o'clock. She wondered if Will was home. Surely Alma wouldn't invite him to their private chat? Or perhaps she would, as a test for Evelyn.

Hayes, the butler, escorted Evelyn into Alma's sitting room at the back of the house. Two small settees, piled with embroidered pillows, sat opposite each other in front of a fireplace. Alma was at a desk along one wall, her back to the door, and continued writing even after Evelyn was announced.

"Please, sit down," Alma ordered without turning around.

Evelyn perched on the edge of one of the settees. A silver tea service and a plate of pastries were arranged on the table in front of her. A cup of tea might help calm her nerves, but she was afraid to break the silence.

After several excruciating minutes, Alma leisurely folded a piece of paper and slid it into an envelope. Then she walked over and took a seat on the settee opposite Evelyn. There was no hug, no greeting. As always, Alma kept herself apart.

"So?" Alma asked as she poured tea into a china cup and passed it to Evelyn. "What is this pressing family matter?"

Evelyn took a deep breath. She must come across as hurt, not angry.

"Charles and I have been married for six months," she began. "As you are aware, we come from very different backgrounds, and I have had much to learn. You and Lavinia have been so gracious. Without your guidance, I would have been quite lost."

The flattery did not soften Alma's suspicious expression.

"I find myself in a very delicate situation, and I hope I can count on your guidance once again."

"Delicate?"

"Yes." Evelyn placed her teacup on the table and looked directly at her mother-in-law. "Nothing would bring me greater happiness than a child. I know it is your fondest wish as well. But Charles is so rarely at home. I find it difficult to do my duty." She refused to lower her gaze, hoping Alma would read her meaning in her eyes.

"Charles is a busy man," Alma said. "Surely you see him in the evenings?"

Evelyn shook her head. "At first, yes. But for the past few months, we've barely crossed paths. He either stays in Baltimore overnight or returns home long after I'm asleep. I don't wish to inconvenience him, yet it seems I must."

"How quickly a doting wife becomes a demanding shrew!" Alma said with a bitter laugh.

"I hope I'm not a shrew," Evelyn said defensively.

Alma picked up the teapot and poured herself a cup, then leisurely stirred in two spoonfuls of sugar. When she continued, her voice was pensive. "It is a delicate balance. A wife must treat her husband as lord and master of the house, yet earn his respect as well. A strong man requires a strong partner."

"What can I do?" Evelyn asked. She heard her voice quaver and prayed she wouldn't cry. Alma considered tears a self-indulgent weakness. "I assure you, I've done nothing to offend him. And yet, I believe Charles has been—that is, I suspect he keeps company with other women."

"He told you?" Alma widened her eyes in horror.

"Not directly. But his disinterest and frequent absences can lead me to no other conclusion."

For a minute, Alma looked as upset as Evelyn. Now that she knew the truth about her son at last, Evelyn hoped she might be an ally after all.

"How dare you raise such a subject in my presence," Alma said, her voice cold with contempt. "Some coarseness is to be expected, given your upbringing. Still, I am appalled."

The words rang through Evelyn's head but she couldn't make sense of them. "Perhaps I wasn't clear—"

"I haven't finished," Alma interrupted, practically spitting out the words. After a brief pause, she continued in her usual calm, measured voice. "I do not approve of such behavior, but it is how things are done. You are very naive indeed if you think a man of Charles's stature can be satisfied with a simple country wife. I trust he's discreet?"

Evelyn stared at Alma, at a loss for words.

"Has he brought a woman to social gatherings? Been seen with someone else by one of your friends?"

Evelyn shook her head. "No, never."

"Then he hasn't embarrassed you in public. Good. Rather than wasting your time on jealousy, think about what has driven him away. If his home were a welcoming haven, Charles would seek it more readily. If he comes home only to be confronted by a suspicious, pouting wife, he'll escape whenever he can. Do you understand?"

"But, I thought, perhaps if you talked to him—"

Alma cut Evelyn off with a quick shake of her head. She lifted her teacup and took a dainty sip before continuing. "As a mother and head of this family, my role is to raise and guide my children. I made sure Charles received the finest education possible, and Lavinia was trained in every aspect of suitable deportment. My children lacked for nothing."

Evelyn noticed that Alma didn't mention Will.

"Finding an appropriate spouse for each child was a matter of the utmost importance," Alma continued. "The future of the family depended on it. I couldn't force a marriage upon my children—nor would I have wanted to—but I could make sure they met and socialized with suitable partners. Both Lavinia and Charles were introduced to society in Philadelphia and New York. I knew they had the looks and breeding to marry into families far above ours.

"Lavinia understood the importance of making the right match. She had her favorite dance partners, of course, and like any young woman she had her head turned by handsome men with no prospects. But these were only passing flirtations. When it came time for marriage, she chose Winslow Preston. Was he the most dashing young man or the richest? No. You can see for yourself that he's rather plodding and dull. But he comes from one of Baltimore's best families, and his honesty has never been questioned. I approved of Winslow from the beginning, and Lavinia could see that he would make a good husband."

Evelyn wondered how much choice Lavinia had had in the matter. Would she have preferred a husband who wouldn't be mistaken for her father? Then again, although Lavinia was certainly pretty, she lacked the confidence to compete in the cutthroat world of New

York heiresses. She looked to Alma for every decision, and if boring old Winslow was her mother's choice, Lavinia would have never dared object.

"Then there was Charles," Alma continued. "He caused a stir wherever he went. He could have married anyone." Her eyes met Evelyn's, and the disapproval in them brought a warm blush to Evelyn's face. "Instead, he chose the daughter of my dressmaker.

"Please understand that I don't mean to insult you," Alma added smoothly. "I merely ask that you consider the situation from my point of view. Charles could have married into any family, and he knew where my preferences lay. He chose to disregard my advice and make a grand gesture of his own. I have no doubt he was infatuated by you. Charles has always longed for what he can't have, ever since he was a child. In many ways, you were the ultimate forbidden prize."

Evelyn reached for her teacup and clutched it with both hands.

"You ask if I can change my son's behavior," Alma went on. "I am the last person whose advice he will heed. If I tell him to do something, he will do the exact opposite to prove his independence."

Evelyn nodded, staring down at her tea. Turning to Alma had been a terrible mistake. Now her mother-in-law knew her marriage was troubled, but would do nothing to help.

"Come now," Alma said, pushing the plate of pastries across the table. "All is not lost. Surely you don't need me to explain the ways a wife may recapture her husband's attentions?"

Evelyn shook off Alma's offer of food. All she could

think of was her disastrous attempt at seduction. The evening that had ended with Will kissing her in the garden.

"Charles is always on the hunt for novelty and amusement," Alma said. "He'd spend more time at home if you offered some diversions."

"A dinner, perhaps?" Evelyn asked.

"That would certainly be appropriate," Alma said. "Only have Charles approve the guest list. You want the right people."

"Yes, of course," Evelyn agreed. "Perhaps even a party. Charles will be turning thirty next month. That calls for a celebration, don't you think?"

"What a charming idea," Alma said. "It must be done right. I would be happy to offer my advice on the menu and decor."

"Thank you. I'm sure Lavinia and Will can help as well." Evelyn blurted out his name without thinking, and saw Alma stiffen at the mention of her older son.

"Lavinia has far more experience entertaining than Will," Alma said. "I wouldn't think his input would be needed."

Once again, Alma's disapproval mystified Evelyn. Will was her eldest child, a man with more charm and kindness than Charles. So why did Alma treat him as a distant, unsavory relative?

There was one possible explanation. Perhaps there was a secret in Will's past, something terrible he kept hidden. The man Evelyn loved might be an illusion. But she couldn't allow herself to believe it. Her whole world— already on shaky ground—would come crashing down.

"Are you certain?" Evelyn asked, keeping her tone

light. "Surely, as Charles's brother, Will should be included in the plans?"

"They may be brothers, but they've never been close," Alma said. "You've seen that for yourself."

"Yet no one has explained the nature of Will's transgressions," Evelyn said. She softened her words with a smile, her expression one of curious innocence.

Alma smiled back, equally insincere. "Will is my son, and I love him," she said. "However, he is irresponsible and has disappointed me on numerous occasions. He takes a passionate interest in one thing for a month, then moves on to another. Nothing lasts. A few years ago, he was engaged to a lovely girl from a fine family. Yet he broke off the engagement with no explanation and disappeared to Europe, leaving us to tidy up his mess. It was mortifying, to say the least.

"When he returned home, I hoped he would embrace his family duty, but I have seen no evidence of it yet. Should he choose to accept a role at Brewster Shipping, marry and settle down, I'm sure all would be forgiven."

Forgiven but never forgotten. Will would always be at Charles's beck and call. His wife would be expected to answer to Alma. Evelyn knew Will would never live under such restrictions.

"Perhaps this party could help reintroduce Will to society," Evelyn suggested.

Alma nodded slowly. "Yes, I think a party might serve all our purposes." Looking at Evelyn intently, she said softly, "I'm not heartless. I remember what it is to wait for a husband who doesn't come home. But feeling sorry for yourself accomplishes nothing. You must lure Charles back. It is the only way."

Alma stood, a clear signal that the meeting was over. "I'll send you some names for the guest list, if that would be helpful."

Standing and nodding goodbye to Alma, Evelyn found herself excited at the thought of going home and starting preparations. Alma was right. She needed something to occupy her time. Frightening as it might be to put together a huge party, it was also an opportunity. A chance to show Charles and Alma that she could live up to the Brewster name. Her feelings for Will wouldn't change, but they could be hidden. For now, her duty was to make Charles happy. Perhaps, if she found the right approach, her husband might even fall in love with her again.

FOUR WHIRLWIND weeks later, the night of the party arrived. Evelyn paused for a moment in the foyer to take stock of it all. Music drifted from the upstairs landing, waiters with trays of champagne circled around women in colorful gowns, the buzz of conversation and laughter enveloped her. Based on the first half hour, the evening was already a triumph.

She turned to Charles, standing beside her near the door. He looked so handsome, with his immaculate tuxedo and confident smile. He greeted his guests with practiced elegance. Evelyn was glad she'd invited a photographer to the house earlier to take their picture. In her elaborate hairstyle and expensive gown, she finally looked worthy of her husband. That moment would be captured forever, a memory of the night when they were the envy of the county.

"What is *she* doing here?" Evelyn heard Alma hiss. Evelyn had initially been annoyed when Alma planted herself in the receiving line next to them, but her mother-in-law had been unexpectedly helpful, whispering names to Evelyn so she could greet her guests properly.

"Who?" Evelyn murmured, peering discreetly down the line to see who Alma found so offensive.

"Lady Dorchester," Alma whispered, putting a disapproving emphasis on the first word. "A title by marriage, not birth. I can't imagine why she was invited."

"Hush, Mother," Charles admonished. "She's staying with the Wiltons, so she had to be included. Ah, good to see you, my boy!" he said, grabbing a slender young man by the hand. He introduced Evelyn to Henry and Alice Wilton, along with their houseguest. Lady Dorchester was shorter and rounder than Evelyn, with bright, lively eyes. Her neck and considerable cleavage were draped in diamonds.

"Who is she?" Evelyn asked, after the guests had moved on.

"She divorced her first husband," Charles said, pursing his lips in disapproval. "That makes her a harlot in Mother's eyes, but her second husband, the duke, is enormously rich and well connected. Not to mention a half-senile invalid. However, a royal title forgives a multitude of sins. Having her at our party could be seen as quite a coup, my dear."

Evelyn smiled and said nothing. It was now acceptable to socialize with a fallen woman? She had much to learn.

"Ah, look who deigned to make an appearance," Charles said. Evelyn turned to see Will walking toward them.

"Happy birthday, Charles," Will said, shaking his brother's hand. "I see you're celebrating in style."

"Indeed. My wife has quite outdone herself."

"So I see." Will turned to Evelyn and took her hand lightly in his. She hoped he would kiss it, but he let go quickly, keeping his distance from her. They'd barely spoken in the past few weeks, other than casual conversation at family dinners. She had done her errands in Baltimore alone, afraid she might weaken if he accompanied her.

"I'm glad you could come," Evelyn said. She smiled warmly to show it was more than polite hostess talk.

"Thank you for keeping your disreputable brother-in-law on the guest list," Will said. He looked around at the crowd. "You did it. Good for you."

Evelyn nodded, glad to have his approval.

"You even look like a Brewster," Will said. Something about his tone made her doubt he intended it as a compliment. Before she could respond, another guest had walked toward her, Charles was making an introduction and Will had disappeared. Even as she pushed aside her disappointment, she was grateful for his discretion. He understood how important this night was for her.

She didn't see Will the rest of the evening. She looked for him occasionally in the throngs of people whose names she still couldn't remember, but she never found him.

Evelyn didn't see much of Charles, either. After leading her in a waltz when the orchestra started playing, Charles joined some of his colleagues for cigars in the conservatory. Evelyn danced with the ancient husbands of Alma's friends, who gave her the admiring glances she'd hoped to receive from Charles.

Still, the party was a success. Evelyn had proved herself to Alma's snobbish friends and Charles's stuffy business acquaintances. Tonight, no one could deny her place here. She was a Brewster at last.

It was well after midnight when guests began to leave. Evelyn stifled a yawn as she stood in the foyer and thanked groups of people for coming.

She motioned to Mr. Trimble, the gardener, who'd been pressed into service retrieving coats and ladies' wraps.

"Have you seen Mr. Brewster?" she asked.

"No, ma'am," he said. "That is—I did see him go upstairs, but that was some time ago."

"Thank you." Evelyn wondered if she should track him down. He wouldn't appreciate her interference, but he was the guest of honor, after all. He should bid his guests farewell personally.

Evelyn made her way upstairs to her bedroom, walking carefully in her voluminous skirt. The lights were off, and the room was empty. She glanced quickly down the hallway, but there was no reason for Charles to be in any of the other rooms. Indeed, she would have gone downstairs without another thought if she hadn't heard an eruption of laughter, a high-pitched sound that she interpreted at first as a muffled scream.

Evelyn took a few steps forward. The lamps hadn't been lit, as this section of the house was rarely used. But in the shadows ahead, she could see the shapes of two figures leaning together against the wall, and something in that silhouette was immediately familiar. She recognized Charles even before he walked toward her out of the darkness.

"Darling!" he exclaimed, taking her hands. His cheeks were flushed, and his voice boomed with unnatural heartiness. "I believe you've met Lady Dorchester."

Despite her reputation, the woman had remarkable poise. She sauntered forward confidently, daring Evelyn to suspect anything. "You have a lovely home, Mrs. Brewster. I simply insisted your husband show me around."

In the dark? Evelyn wanted to shout her accusations at the pair of them. But she had no proof, merely a glimpse of two people standing too close in a deserted corridor.

"Charles, it has been a pleasure," Lady Dorchester said, kissing him lightly on the cheek. "It's time you tended to your wife. She looks exhausted." Lady Dorchester's mocking laugh echoed in Evelyn's head even as she turned and ran to her bedroom. That laughter was the sound of victory.

Downstairs, a single violin was playing. The chattering of voices had softened to a gentle hum. Evelyn knew she should be standing by the front door, graciously seeing off her guests. Even now, they would be wondering why their hosts had disappeared. Her absence would cast a pall over an otherwise perfect evening.

But Evelyn couldn't face them. This party, intended to save her marriage, had instead revealed its true nature. Charles would play the faithful husband in public, even escort her across a dance floor from time to time. But in the shadows, out of sight, he would give himself up to temptation. He had so little respect for his wife that he would insult her in her own home. If this was the future of her marriage, she didn't see how she could bear it.

Only one thing might help her get through this night. Wiping away her tears, Evelyn pulled herself upright and opened the drawer of her bedside table, where she kept a box of monogrammed stationery. Will had told her to write if she ever needed him. Now, she wanted nothing more than to pour out her feelings to him. Will would not expect her to meekly accept the situation. Will, she realized, was the only person who might be able to think of a way out.

CHAPTER NINE

ALISSA AND DANNY drove past the winding driveway of Roger Blake's house twice before they found it. From the road, the house was hidden behind trees and giant shrubs, a secretive location that only reinforced Alissa's doubts about the man. When she'd called to ask about his book on unsolved crimes, he'd insisted they talk in person, refusing to give any specifics over the phone.

"Maybe he's one of those wackos who thinks his line is tapped," Alissa told Danny afterward.

"You want me to come with you?" Danny offered. "I'm sure he's harmless, but if it would make you feel better…"

"It's probably a waste of time," Alissa protested. But at the thought of Danny at her side, her misgivings about the trip faded. "But you're welcome to tag along."

As Danny steered his truck along the twisting country roads, Alissa was glad she'd accepted his suggestion. Danny drove with the relaxed ease of someone who had traveled these routes countless times before, and Alissa was free to daydream as they sped past fields dotted with wildflowers. After they finally tracked down Roger's house and parked in the driveway, Alissa was reassured by the building's immaculate white clapboard facade and bright red shutters. Flowers had been planted in neat rows on either side of the path leading to the front door. It certainly didn't look like the home of an unstable conspiracy theorist.

Roger Blake turned out to be nothing like she'd expected. Instead of a twitchy, nervous eccentric, pale from lack of sunlight, the man who opened the door looked healthy and vigorous. He wasn't much older than Alissa, with thick auburn hair and the ruddy complexion of someone who spent time outside. He flashed a delighted smile and grabbed her hand with a firm grip.

"Alissa. So glad you came. Such a pleasure."

Alissa turned to Danny. "This is Danny Pierce, my, uh…" She was about to say "friend," but stopped abruptly. It might give Roger the wrong idea.

"Handyman," Danny said with a smile.

"He's helping renovate my house," Alissa explained. "The one where the Brewsters used to live."

"Come in, come in," Roger urged.

Alissa and Danny followed him down a short hallway and into a large room filled with well-worn armchairs and a mismatched assortment of side tables. But what caught Alissa's attention immediately were the piles of papers covering every flat surface. Roger was clearly a man obsessed by his work. Alissa wondered if he'd insisted she visit because he was starved for human contact. Danny flashed Alissa a look that seemed to say, "This guy's crazy."

"I'm so sorry," Roger apologized, pushing a stack of books off one side of a couch. "Please, sit. I've made iced tea—would you like some?"

"Sure," Alissa said. As Roger disappeared into the

kitchen, she squeezed into the narrow open space on the sofa and glanced at the books piled next to her. *Jack the Ripper: Case Closed. Shakespeare: Man or Myth? Crime and Punishment in Medieval Europe.* Danny carefully lifted a pile of folders off a chair across from her and placed them on the floor so he could sit. He raised his eyebrows at Alissa, and she shrugged.

"I hope ginger-peach is all right," Roger said, emerging with three cut-glass goblets. "I've had to give up caffeine completely. I was downing coffee like you wouldn't believe, and then I wasn't sleeping, and things were getting a little shaky, so I went cold turkey." If Roger was this chatty decaffeinated, Alissa wondered what he'd been like before.

"Tastes great," she said, taking a sip.

Roger smiled with delight, as if she'd given him an extravagant compliment.

"So," Danny said, anxious to get to the point. "The Brewsters."

"Yes, yes, yes," Roger said as he settled down in a worn recliner. "That house is a treasure. I had a look around a few months ago, and I was overwhelmed by its aura. The sense of history."

"I felt that way myself," Alissa agreed.

"It's got to be a huge project, fixing it up. Good thing you've got experience in that kind of thing."

In their brief phone call, Alissa hadn't told Roger she was a designer. He must have been checking up on her. She found the idea unsettling, but supposed she shouldn't have been surprised.

"I'm lucky enough to have Danny," Alissa said. "He's been doing the brunt of the work."

Danny shook his head, brushing off the compliment. "Your book," he reminded Roger.

Roger leaned forward. "Listen, I'll be honest with both of you. This book may be my masterpiece. I'm not embarrassed to tell you it's been a struggle to figure out what I'm meant to do. I started out thinking I was going to be the next Edgar Allan Poe. But all I could write were bad imitations of Gothic novels. By then, though, I'd gotten caught up in the history of the nineteenth century, so I decided that was my calling. I got halfway through my Ph.D. when I couldn't take it anymore.

"I devoted myself to writing full-time. You might have seen my gardening column in the *Baltimore Sun*? No, well, I suppose you're too busy with the house. But my real passion is true crime. Not the trashy modern stuff—I explore older cases, sort of combining both my interests. Through the garden column, I've met all these marvelous old ladies who've lived around here forever, and they've been filling me in on local history. I've got the makings of a fantastic book."

Danny sighed in frustration. Obviously, this windbag was drawing out his story, reveling in their attention. He wondered if Alissa was regretting this visit, though she continued to nod encouragingly. Her patience was one of the things Danny had grown to admire. Renovating a house meant confronting all sorts of unexpected challenges—from spilled paint to leaky ceilings—but each setback only made Alissa work harder. He was sometimes awed by her determination.

"The Brewsters weren't on my radar screen originally," Roger rambled on. "Charles Brewster's death was an accident, not a crime. Tragic and all that, but straightforward. I only became suspicious after I came across something in the Baltimore Police Department archives. I went there originally to research another case—Henry Wallace, who was suspected of poisoning his wife. Ever heard of him? It was quite a sensation in the 1890s. He was put on trial, but acquitted, partly because it was never proven that his wife had been poisoned at all. It was only later that they discovered he'd been having an affair for years, which gave him a motive.

"I thought, using modern forensic techniques, I might be able to discover whether the wife had been poisoned. That meant finding her original autopsy report in the police archives. You should see those records—stuffed in boxes, things from different years all piled together. It's a disgrace. So, as I was looking through them, I came across a very curious document. A memoir by a policeman named Hyram Haycroft. Apparently, he wrote it for his family—to document his glorious career—and one of his kids gave a copy to the police department so his legend would live on."

Danny shifted his legs, openly bored by Roger's digressions. Alissa hoped Roger would get the hint.

"Anyway," Roger continued, "this Detective Haycroft was one of the top guys in the Baltimore Police Department when he retired. I flipped through the pages, just to see what was there, and I found something interesting at the very beginning. He started out as a policeman in Oak Hill. Ah, I've piqued your curiosity now, haven't I? Here, let me read you his exact words."

Roger reached toward the side table next to him and pulled a few photocopied pages from a red folder.

"'The first victim of violent death I ever saw was Charles Brewster,'" Roger read in a deep, dramatic voice, clearly loving the intrigue. "'As a young man of barely twenty-one, it made a strong impression on me. The Brewsters were the grandest family in town, and the death of their son and heir was a terrible blow. I have seen other deaths from falls since then, and the effect of the broken body is always chilling. My superior, Officer Petry, emphasized the importance of discretion when investigating such a death. Officer Petry performed an initial examination of the body, while I attended to Mr. Brewster's young wife. She was more self-contained than I would have expected, but I would often see such a reaction in the years to follow. The reality is so horrifying that the loved one is struck dumb by shock, showing no emotion for hours or even days afterward. I was spared the ordeal of breaking the news to the rest of the Brewster family, as Officer Petry took on that sad duty. I was left to stand watch over Mr. Brewster's body, and I was curious to discover a gun not ten feet from where he lay.

"'However, when I brought my findings to Officer Petry, he cautioned me against drawing conclusions too readily. The gun was soon identified by his wife as Mr. Brewster's, not that of an intruder, and in any case, it was unrelated to the cause of death. In deference to the family, the gun could be disregarded. Nothing could be gained by the suggestion that Charles Brewster took his own life.'"

Roger flashed Alissa a triumphant look. "Well?"

Alissa could imagine the scene. Charles's battered body, a gun not far away. Evelyn strangely composed.

There was no mention of where the body was found. Was it in the foyer?

"It seems pretty clear to me," Danny said. "Charles committed suicide."

Roger shrugged. "Well, Detective Haycroft thought it was a possibility. Which would certainly make a good story. Why would Charles Brewster, with his great house and beautiful wife, be miserable enough to kill himself? But don't you think there's something off about the whole scenario? It's not as if there was an autopsy. I'll bet you anything Charles Brewster's body was carted off to the mansion and cleaned up by some poor servant. That's how they did it in those days. Do you think anyone checked for bullet holes?"

Alissa gulped down a mouthful of tea, hoping the cold sting would distract her from the image of Charles's ruined body. She glanced at Danny, who was now listening intently.

"And how about that description of Mrs. Brewster? 'More self-contained than I would have expected.' Granted, she was in shock, but this policeman thought there was something strange about her. You'd think she'd be crying or fainting. Instead, she's calmly identifying her husband's gun, but not offering any explanation for why it would be there. It's all very strange."

"That hardly means she murdered her husband," Alissa insisted, oddly offended on Evelyn's behalf.

"Look at the evidence," Roger said. "A young woman with no money marries into this rich family. Who knows—maybe Charles isn't quite what she imagined. Maybe she's got some other guy on the side. But what's really suspicious is her behavior after her husband's death. She's got this great house and the Brewster name, which means she's set for life, and what does she do? She disappears. Doesn't that strike you as weird?"

"You never know how someone will respond to a loss like that," Danny argued. Something in his voice made Alissa wonder if he was speaking from personal experience.

"Maybe Evelyn couldn't stand living in the house where Charles died," Alissa suggested.

"Sure, but why leave town? She would've had it made, as the widow of Charles Brewster. Remember, this was a girl who came from nothing. She'd lived her whole life in Oak Hill. Where would she go?"

For that, Alissa had no answer.

"FORGET THE GARDENING columns, that guy needs to write a murder mystery," Danny said as they began the ride home. "Talk about an active imagination."

"You don't think he might be on to something?" Alissa asked. She kept flashing back to an image of a bloody body lying in the foyer. Could Evelyn have come up behind Charles, held a gun to his head, pulled the trigger and watched his body tumble over the edge? Or even just threatened him with the gun and forced him to jump? She had a hard time picturing the shy girl in that wedding photo as a scheming killer.

"Roger Blake is a classic small-town busybody," Danny said dismissively. "He doesn't have a life of his own, so he comes up with these stories to make himself feel important. He got your attention, didn't he? That's all he was after."

"Is that what people in small towns want?" Alissa asked wryly. "Attention from us sophisticated city folk?"

"I hate to break it to you, but you live in Oak Hill," Danny said. "You're a small-town girl now, whether you like it or not."

Their easy rapport gave Alissa the confidence to steer the conversation in a more personal direction. "Why do you live out here?" she asked him. "You said you went to Georgetown, got an MBA..."

"In other words, why don't I run a multinational corporation and rake in the big bucks?" he asked.

"Something like that." Alissa had felt drawn to him from the minute he'd arrived at her door, but she was still unsettled by how little she really knew about him. If she could get him to open up to her now, maybe she'd be able to tell if they had a shot at something more.

"Well, I grew up in Oak Hill," Danny began. "I was considered the smart kid in the family, so my parents always expected me to go off and make something of myself. I thought my dad would understand when I majored in art history—he and I spent hours carving wood scraps in the garage when I was a kid—but he wasn't exactly thrilled. I got a scholarship to study abroad, and I went all over Europe, seeing everything I could. It's like I knew it was the only chance I'd get."

Danny smoothly shifted the truck's gears as they merged onto the highway. "When I came home, I applied to a bunch of business schools. Not because I particularly wanted to go, but I couldn't think what else to do. My mom just about fainted with excitement when I got into Georgetown, so that decided it. The day after graduation, I started at an investment bank on Wall Street. I was the only person they hired out of a hundred interviews. I'm still not sure why they chose me—I guess they saw I was willing to give up everything for the job. Which I did, for a while. But it didn't work out."

He said it so casually, as if that prestigious career was no more than a hobby he'd tried halfheartedly before dropping. Alissa trusted Danny completely when it came to the house—he'd proved himself a dedicated worker. But there was something not quite settled about him, a part that remained detached and out of reach. If he disappeared without a trace one day, she wouldn't be entirely surprised.

"What happened?" Alissa asked.

"Hang on," Danny interrupted. "There's something I want to show you." The truck began to slow, although Alissa couldn't see an exit ramp. When Danny pulled off onto the shoulder, there was nothing but open land on either side of the road.

"Roll down your window," Danny urged. He leaned across her, pointing outside.

Alissa looked out across the overgrown grass. They were stopped on a hill, and Alissa could see a collection of dollhouse-sized buildings in the distance below. She recognized the steeple of a church and realized she was staring at Oak Hill.

"Oh!" Alissa exclaimed. "I didn't know we were so close."

"See that row of pine trees to the left?" Danny asked. "That's the end of your property." The house itself was obscured by vegetation at this distance, but Alissa recognized the line of neatly spaced evergreens.

"Believe it or not," Danny said, "this is the site of the original Brewster mansion."

"Really?" Alissa tried to picture the house Elaine Price and Julia Larkin had described, with imposing stone walls and turrets that loomed over the countryside. Grass and asphalt had covered any trace of it.

"They could look out over the town and their land from up here," Danny said.

"How did you know where it was?" Alissa asked.

"Your curiosity must've rubbed off on me," Danny said. "I've been looking over some old county maps stashed away in my parents' garage. Trying to get a sense of what it was like around here years ago."

"Just make sure you don't get obsessed," Alissa teased.

She expected Danny to toss back a flippant reply, but he said nothing as he stared out the window. If he'd been a different kind of person, Alissa would have guessed he was daydreaming, as she so often did. But Danny wasn't the type to lose himself in fantasies. The trip to Roger's and this stop along the highway were his peace offerings to her. An apology for making fun of her fascination with the Brewsters.

They sat side by side in the front of the truck, their silence interrupted only by the intermittent hum of passing cars. All day, Alissa realized, she'd related to Danny as a friend rather than an employee. His insistence on treating her as the boss seemed to have softened. Was he starting to see her as something more?

"We'd better get back," Danny said, shifting the car into Drive. "I want to get back on the clock by noon."

"I'll pay you for the whole day, don't worry," Alissa said.

Danny stiffened, and he hit the accelerator. "I offered to come to Roger's with you," he said. "Pay me for the hours I work, okay?"

Alissa searched for words to put things right, but she could tell by the way Danny kept his eyes on the road, his mouth pressed in a tight line, that she had stumbled into dangerous territory. She'd intended to be kind by paying for his time this morning. There was no reason he should suffer because of her obsession. She realized now, too late, that her offer had cheapened the whole outing, turning a friendly trip into a commercial transaction. She wished she could apologize but anything she said would only make matters worse.

They drove the rest of the way home without speaking. As they pulled into the driveway, Alissa saw a tall rectangular package leaning against the front door.

"Did you order something?" Alissa asked.

Danny shook his head, apparently as confused as she was.

He helped her carry the box inside and pulled out a pocketknife to slit it open. Alissa pushed back the cardboard and layers of bubble wrap, and suddenly she was eye-to-eye with Charles Brewster, who was staring at her as if from the dead. Next to him stood Evelyn, curls framing her face, her features as delicate as the flowers that decorated her dress.

It was the party photograph she'd scanned at the library. Reproduced and enlarged, ready to be hung on the wall to commemorate the Brewsters' love. But now, thanks to Roger, Alissa couldn't look at them without a sense of dread. Had Charles been as pleased with himself as he appeared, or was he putting a brave face over some secret anguish? And if Roger was right, Evelyn hadn't been the loving wife she appeared. She looked off to the side, away from her husband, as if she couldn't face what she was about to do to him.

Or maybe they'd been exactly what they seemed to be: a young couple who thought their lives were just beginning. Two people with no idea of the tragedy looming ahead.

"You okay?" Danny asked. His voice dragged her back to the present.

"Yeah," Alissa said, but she knew her voice betrayed her.

"Is this the picture you're going to hang in the living room?" Danny asked.

"I was," Alissa said. "Now I'm not sure."

Danny shrugged. "This is your place now. There's no reason it should be a shrine to the Brewsters."

"That wasn't my goal," Alissa said, but in a way, it had been. She thought by recreating the Brewsters' house, she might recapture some of their glamour, and maybe some of their happiness would rub off on her. After talking to Roger, their lives didn't appear so enviable.

Danny sensed her disappointment, and he wanted to tell her he understood. He'd gotten caught up in her curiosity about the house's history. But the way she was talking now, her voice a monotone, made it clear she wanted to be left alone. She didn't trust him enough to share what she was really thinking.

"I'm going to rip out the last of those kitchen cabinets," Danny said. "You can take a look at the new drawer pulls when you get a chance."

Alissa half expected him to call her ma'am. The comfortable give-and-take of their earlier conversation had been replaced by this impersonal exchange. Danny presented himself as such an uncomplicated, regular guy—the hunky handyman, as Constance kept calling him—that Alissa was intrigued when he revealed something deeper. She'd glimpsed another side of him today, a willingness to help and support her despite his own misgivings. She couldn't let that connection slip away.

"You know, I was thinking," she burst out. "Would you like to have dinner sometime?"

The invitation was so impulsive that the words surprised her even as she said them. "I just thought," she went on, "it would be nice to talk when we're relaxed and showered and not stressed-out about work. Not like a date or anything!" she added with a nervous laugh.

Why had she said that? Because when she thought about having dinner with Danny, she imagined it as a date. Glasses of wine, flirting over dessert, a walk to her front door ending in...what?

Danny smiled. "Is tomorrow good?"

"Sure." Alissa glanced away to hide her giddy excitement and found herself looking once again at Evelyn Brewster's wistful face. She was a woman who had everything. So why didn't she look happier?

CHAPTER TEN

"THEY WILL DESTROY YOU."

Katherine O'Keefe held her daughter's hands as they sat in her small front parlor. This space, which had seemed so large to Evelyn as a child, now felt cramped. She noticed the worn patches on the chairs' upholstery and the scrapes on the wood cabinet. Already, it seemed, she regarded the world with a Brewster perspective. She could look at this room, once her haven, and see only its shabbiness.

Katherine repeated her warning. "That's exactly what he said. They will destroy you."

Evelyn had been too afraid to meet with a lawyer herself in case word got back to Alma or Charles, so she asked her mother to make inquiries. She could not bear to confess what had happened at the party—the humiliation of that woman laughing at her, mocking her in her own house—but she revealed her suspicions that Brewster Shipping was losing money. The firm's instability, she said, intensified Charles's moodiness and his appetite for liquor. She spoke of her dread on those nights, ever more frequent, when he stormed through the front door, drunk and belligerent. Unhappiness wasn't grounds for divorce, she told her mother, but fear of her husband might be.

Katherine had promised to be discreet. She took the train to Philadelphia, where she met with the friend of a distant cousin who had a law practice. Evelyn knew her mother strongly disapproved of divorce. It was a measure of how much Katherine loved her daughter that she agreed to help, despite her misgivings.

"I didn't mention names, as you requested," Katherine said, "only that I was asking on behalf of a woman who'd married into a prominent family with friends in the government. He said that judges would inevitably favor a family with social connections over a young woman of no status. If Charles objected, the judge would refuse to grant the divorce. You would remain a Brewster but your reputation would be ruined. He was quite clear on that."

"Suppose I didn't care about my reputation and continued petitioning. Would a divorce ever be granted?"

"If you were in grave physical danger, perhaps," Katherine said. "A wife who has been maimed by her husband might convince a judge to release her. But in most cases, if a husband chooses to deny a divorce, the law sides with him. A wife may attempt to argue her case to a higher court, but that takes money. And the moment a wife begins divorce proceedings, the husband is under no obligation to support her."

"I don't want his money," Evelyn said.

"Easy to say now," Katherine said. "You're well fed, and in good health. But you're not the only one who would lose everything."

Evelyn nodded. If she took on the Brewsters, her mother would be tainted as well. No one in town would hire her as a dressmaker. They would both be shunned by society, forced to move away. Could she scrape together enough money to start over? Charles gave her a meager allowance. Even if she saved all of it for the next few months, it wouldn't be much of a nest egg.

"My heart aches for you." Katherine wrapped an arm around Evelyn's shoulders and pulled her close. "But perhaps you can make the best of a bad situation."

"Perhaps."

Evelyn had prepared herself for the shame of a divorce. But she hadn't realized the odds would be so stacked against her. Charles could refuse the divorce and she would remain Mrs. Brewster, at his mercy in the eyes of the law. He would never forgive her for exposing his family to scandal. How would he take his revenge?

"All is not lost, surely?" Katherine asked. "You won't change him, but you could change your expectations. Ignore your husband's indiscretions. Once you have a child, his behavior might improve."

"Yes, a child," Evelyn said. She'd told her mother Charles no longer shared her bed. Couldn't she see that a child was less likely now than ever?

"In any case, there's no need to rush matters," Katherine said. "Make sure you know what you're doing before you take such a drastic step."

Evelyn nodded. "I'd hoped it would be easier."

Katherine hugged Evelyn closer, one hand stroking her daughter's hair as she used to do years ago. "I wish I could make it all better," she whispered.

"I know." But Evelyn had gotten herself into this mess by marrying Charles Brewster. She would have to save herself.

Evelyn walked home slowly, depression weighing down each step. The days stretched out before her, hopeless and unchanging. Charles was in New York on business, which was a relief, but Will was gone as well, to Baltimore for a few days. There would be nothing waiting for her under the garden bench today. For the past few weeks, ever since the night of Charles's birthday party, Evelyn and Will had left messages for each other in the garden, notes that had become her lifeline. It began with the letter she wrote him the night of the ball, a cry for help as she reeled from her husband's betrayal. She'd hidden it in the garden the next morning, wondering how long it would take Will to find it.

To her surprise, she found an envelope waiting for her when she looked under the bench the following day. Will's handwriting was a rushed scrawl, as if he knew how anxiously she was awaiting his reply.

My dearest Evelyn,
*   What a sordid end to a splendid evening! Don't you realize you are in fine company? All the best wives in America and Europe have found Lady Dorchester hanging off their husbands. Indeed, you have entered a most exclusive sisterhood...*

She read on, smiling at his irreverence. She knew Will would find a way to lessen the sting. It was one of the things she loved most about him.

Later that evening, Charles informed her that he would be moving into one of the guest bedrooms.

"This way I won't disturb you with my comings and goings late at night," he explained.

"But, if we want a child…" she began.

"Enough!" he snapped, all pretense of calm and politeness vanishing. "I am well aware of the need for a precious Brewster heir!"

The following night, Evelyn was startled when the bedroom door flew open. Charles stood in the doorway, his face flushed.

"Wake up!" he commanded. As he swaggered toward the bed, Evelyn took in his grim expression and tried to turn away. He slapped her face and she bit her lip to keep from crying out.

"Isn't this what you wanted?" he shouted.

The nightmare was mercifully brief. Charles pounced on her like an animal attacking its prey. She swallowed her screams, terrified that any sound might infuriate him more, and endured the pain. Suddenly, Charles collapsed. He took a few ragged breaths, then pulled himself off her. She kept her eyes clenched shut, afraid to see the triumph in his face.

But when he spoke, she heard appalled bewilderment.

"Good God," he murmured. "You drive me to such a state, Evelyn." He sighed, and she felt the bed shift as he settled next to her. "I don't think I did you a great favor by marrying you. It's all gone wrong since then. Brewster Shipping is losing money, the dockhands are threatening to strike, tenants are grumbling whenever I raise their rents… You can't understand the burdens I have to bear. I come home, to the place that should be my sanctuary, and do you know what I feel? Disappointment."

Evelyn lay still, her body turned away from him. If Charles was willing to apologize for his behavior, she would listen. But she would not forgive. Not yet.

"Nothing in my life has gone as hoped," Charles said. "My passion for you blinded me to how unsuitable we are. You could never be the sort of wife I need—how could you be, a girl from Oak Hill who has seen nothing of the world? I thought I glimpsed something more in you, some impertinent spark that intrigued me. But it's gone. You no longer excite me. I'm prepared to do my duty as a husband, but I won't tolerate accusations or demands. You are my wife, and you will obey. Don't provoke me, and tonight's events don't need to be repeated."

Evelyn didn't respond. Silence was the only weapon she had left.

After a few minutes, Charles rose and left the room. Evelyn lay in bed, exhausted and yet unable to sleep. Much as she longed for a baby, she prayed that she wouldn't conceive now. No child deserved to be born from such violence.

As the sunlight slowly filtered into the bedroom, Evelyn realized it was Sunday. She and Charles were expected at Alma's for dinner. She dragged herself out of bed and stood in front of the mirror at her dressing table. Her cheeks were raw from the force of Charles's blows, and she had a bruise under one eye. The throbbing ache between her legs made walking painful.

When Peggy arrived with breakfast, Evelyn asked her to tell Charles that she was unwell and would remain in her room for the day. Charles didn't come to check on her, for which she was grateful. Seeing him in the light of day, immaculate and unrepentant, might have sent her over the edge.

She tried to sleep, tried to read, but could only brood

over what had happened. When she was sure Charles had left for Alma's, she pulled out her stationery and began a letter to Will.

I am so sorry I had to miss dinner today. Did you miss my sparkling conversation?

She stopped, tore up the paper and started again.

I eagerly await the highlights of today's dinner. Did Winslow recount another dull tale of his school days?

She stared at the words. Try as she might, she couldn't be amusing today.

She took out a fresh sheet of paper and began once again, this time writing from the heart. She described how Charles had attacked her, and how she feared he would hurt her again. She begged Will not to confront his brother, as it would only make things worse. *Simply telling you has already brought me some relief,* she wrote.

Evelyn pulled a robe over her nightgown, slipped on a pair of shoes and limped downstairs. She saw Mrs. Trimble walking toward her across the foyer, carrying a tray of food. The housekeeper's usually impassive face flickered with vague surprise.

"Mr. Brewster left instructions that you were to be attended in your room," she said.

"What are you doing here?" Evelyn demanded. Although Peggy and Mrs. Gower had only Sunday evenings off, Mrs. Trimble and her husband were given the entire day.

"Mr. Brewster asked me to care for you." Mrs. Trimble peered at the welts on Evelyn's face. "He said you had a fever."

"Yes." Evelyn turned away so the woman couldn't get a closer look. "I came down for some fresh air. I think a short stroll in the garden will do me good."

"Shall I accompany you?"

"I won't be more than a few minutes," Evelyn said. "Could you have tea ready when I return?"

"Yes, ma'am."

That would get her out of the way for a short time, at least. Evelyn walked outside and caught her breath as a chilly breeze hit her. Soon, it would be too cold to walk outside. What excuse would she have for retrieving Will's messages? She couldn't bear the thought of months without them.

Then, suddenly, Will was there in person, standing in front of her. He grinned as he walked toward her. "Ah, Juliet…" he began. His words trailed off as he moved closer and saw her more clearly. He reached out his hands, then stopped, as if touching her might cause pain.

"What happened?" he asked.

"It's all here," Evelyn said, holding out the note. "I was going to leave it for you under the bench." She turned her face downward, self-conscious of how she must look to him.

"Did Charles do this?" Will asked.

Evelyn had been able to write everything down, but she wasn't strong enough to say it out loud. Not yet.

"My God," he murmured. "I never dreamed it was as bad as that."

"Neither did I," Evelyn said.

Will took a step toward her, but she pulled back. "Mrs. Trimble's in the kitchen. She mustn't see us."

"Come with me." He put one hand on her elbow, ready to escort her to their secret place in the private garden. Evelyn pulled away again.

"No, you have to go," she said. "Charles told her to keep an eye on me. He can't know you were here."

"He won't. I'll go," Will said.

"Please, just promise you'll keep writing," Evelyn begged. "It's such a comfort."

Will took the letter from her and brushed his lips along her forehead, more a caress than kiss. "Be careful," he said. Then he turned and slipped away through the hedges.

Will might have joked once of being her Romeo, but he was no impetuous boy. He didn't challenge Charles to a duel, or whisk Evelyn off in a daring rescue. He simply wrote to her as a friend, offering support and sympathy. At times she wished for the distraction of a love letter, hoping Will would acknowledge the longing they both felt. But mostly she was grateful for his discretion. Romantic dreams would only make her situation more impossible.

Will was the one who first raised the possibility of her leaving Charles. He reassured Evelyn that divorce no longer meant social suicide—many divorcées were still received by the best families in New York, including the infamous Lady Dorchester. Evelyn never would have consulted a lawyer without his encouragement. But on the day Katherine went to Philadelphia for the consultation, Will left a note saying he'd gone to visit an old friend in Baltimore for a few days.

It felt like years. She hadn't realized until then how much she depended on his notes. She would wake up in the morning and wonder when to make her trip to the garden. After breakfast? Or wait until afternoon to prolong the anticipation? She would read Will's letters over and over. After nightfall, she would sneak outside and hide her reply, her pulse racing as she tried to avoid the servants. These exchanges brought a thrill to her stifling, unchanging routine.

Now, as she walked home from her mother's, she wondered how to tell Will that a divorce might be impossible. When she entered the house, she saw an envelope addressed to her, propped up on the table next to the door.

She pulled out a small rectangular card.

10 p.m.

No name, no place. But she knew the handwriting. Will would be waiting for her tonight in the garden.

That evening, as she trod through the dark, silent house with only a candle to guide her, Evelyn's heart thumped with nervous excitement. It was the same way she'd felt when Charles began flirting with her, a year ago. A lifetime ago. It had all seemed like such an adventure then. She'd been in love with the idea of love. But her feelings had nothing to do with Charles himself.

Now, with Will, Evelyn knew the difference. Her love for him had bloomed because of who he was: a man who looked at the world with optimism and hope. Someone who made happiness seem possible. If meeting Will was the only good to come of her marriage to Charles, perhaps everything else was worth it.

"Evelyn!"

She rushed through the opening in the hedge at the sound of his voice. Her eyes took a few moments to adjust to the darkness. Will was there, in front of her, his gaze meeting hers over the flame of the candle. Then he blew it out. Their arms found each other, and they clung together. His breath warmed her neck.

"Come, sit," he said, pulling Evelyn toward the bench. She drew her shawl tight around her shoulders and nestled in next to him.

"I had to see you," Will confessed.

"When did you get back?" Evelyn asked.

"This afternoon. I left the note at your house as soon as I returned."

"I have news," Evelyn said before he could continue, wanting to get the worst over with. "It's not encouraging. My mother talked to a lawyer about the divorce. I'm not worried about my reputation, but the lawyer says I'll have very little recourse if Charles refuses, which I have no doubt he will. I don't have the money to fight him in court."

Will watched her impassively. Perhaps he'd expected this outcome.

"So, I need to find another solution," Evelyn went on. "I thought Charles might agree to a separation instead of a divorce. Many couples make that sort of arrangement."

"Is that what you want?" Will asked. "An arrangement?"

"Of course not," Evelyn said indignantly.

"Neither do I." Will sighed. He reached over and intertwined his fingers with hers. "Do you know what

I really want?" he asked. "I want you to divorce Charles and marry me."

The declaration was so unexpected, so heartfelt, that Evelyn couldn't help smiling.

"Is the idea so ridiculous?" Will asked.

"No, no," Evelyn protested. "It's not every day a married woman receives a proposal."

"Then we're agreed?"

"There's nothing I want more," Evelyn said. "Only— you make it sound so simple."

"It is."

Evelyn felt Will's hand against her cheek, turning her face toward his. Then they were kissing with an intensity that shattered all her doubts. This was how it was meant to be. She could battle any obstacle if she knew Will was waiting for her on the other side.

"We *are* agreed, then," he murmured.

"What about Charles?" Evelyn asked. Just saying his name brought back the churning fear. "He won't let me go easily. Your family will disown you if you take my side. Even if we ran off together, how would we support ourselves?"

Will gently put a finger to her lips to silence the panic. "Being disowned doesn't scare me. I've been the family's black sheep long enough."

"Because of the canceled engagement?"

"It goes back much further. I'm not really a Brewster, never have been."

"What do you mean?" Evelyn asked.

"I'm the product of my mother's first marriage," Will said.

"Alma was married before?" Evelyn asked, amazed.

"Yes, though she's done her best to cover it up," Will said. "She doesn't come from a grand family, you know. She always wanted to move up in the world. My real father was a young minister in Baltimore. Not a very lucrative profession, but he was a respectable man with a promising future. She set her sights on him, and they married a few months after meeting. She was pregnant with me when he died. Struck by a carriage in front of their house. Even I can manage some pity for her then— a young widow expecting a child on her own.

"Only someone like Mother could have gone from such tragedy to social triumph. Edward Brewster was a member of my father's congregation. I imagine Mother sorted through her prospects, found the richest man she could and set out to catch him. She must've put on quite a show—the poor young widow looking for a protector. They were married soon after I was born, and had Charles the following year.

"There must be a few old biddies in Baltimore who know the truth and still consider Mother an upstart social climber, but no one dares cross her now. Once Edward adopted me, she considered our past erased. Unfortunately, I was a constant reminder of her humble beginnings. Charles was the real Brewster, the favored son. I did my best to fit in. I went to the finest schools with the other spoiled brats, but I always knew I was different. Charles did, too. He took every opportunity to remind me that I didn't have Brewster blood. And I don't. Try as I might, I couldn't summon any interest in shipping or social climbing. My parents never forgave me for it.

"If they were going to disapprove of me anyway, I

thought, why not give them good reason? What better revenge than to jilt the girl they had pushed on me and leave the country? How very un-Brewster, to go off and enjoy myself! Mother's scolding letters followed me across Europe, but Father never cut off my funds, as I thought he would. Officially, he disapproved enormously, but I think he also envied me, living as I wished.

"However, the years of wandering eventually took their toll. I was tired of always being a stranger, starting over every few months. I even missed my parents' awful house, if you can believe it! I thought that perhaps, after Father died, Mother and I might start over. But I came home to find I was still the disreputable brother, forever in Charles's shadow. Nothing had changed. Except you."

Evelyn leaned over to kiss him, trying to soothe the lingering pain. His lips clung hungrily to hers, and they kissed with a desperate intensity. Will's hands slipped inside her shawl and she led them to her neckline, her skin tingling as he traced his fingers along her shoulders and throat. When they first met, Evelyn had been drawn to Will's way with words. Tonight, she glimpsed another side to him, a man who could weaken her without saying anything.

But she didn't go further than a kiss, especially now that freedom was within reach. No matter what mud Charles and the Brewsters flung at her, she wouldn't care. She could survive Charles's rage if Will was her reward. There would be time enough for passion later.

CHAPTER ELEVEN

IT'S NOT A DATE, Alissa told herself. Still, she circled back to the mirror to check her reflection more than once before leaving the bedroom.

"I know this great little place in the middle of nowhere," Danny had suggested. "Simple but good."

The restaurant might be simple, but Alissa decided her outfit wouldn't be. Danny saw her in jeans every day; if nothing else, this dinner would give her an excuse to pull out some of the stylish clothes she used to wear to work. She chose a figure-enhancing knit wrap dress and mid-heel sandals: dressy but not desperate. She tousled her hair in a vain attempt to give it some curl, then gave up and pulled it back in a low ponytail. After applying some makeup—mascara and lipstick, nothing too obvious—she went downstairs to wait on the front porch.

Danny was driving up as she stepped outside. The flatbed of his pickup was littered with paint cans and jumbled piles of wood, but the cab was immaculate.

"Hey there," said Danny as Alissa stepped inside. He glanced quickly from her head to her feet, then back again. "You look nice."

"Thanks." Pleased as she was to have her effort acknowledged, she wasn't sure how to respond. *It's dinner,* she reminded herself, *nothing more.*

After driving about fifteen minutes out of town, Alissa saw a red neon sign for Jack's Place at a bend in the road. Inside, a counter ran along one side of the room, complete with old-timers who looked as if they'd been hunched there for decades. Booths with worn brown leather seats were scattered through the rest of the space. Alissa scanned the clientele and realized she was the only person wearing something other than jeans or shorts.

"Hey, Danny," said a teenage girl standing near the door. She wore her hair in two long braids, and her braces glinted in the light when she smiled.

"Alissa, this is Kim," Danny said. "Her dad's the owner and chef. I've known them forever."

"The usual seat?" Kim asked Danny. When he nodded, she picked up two menus from the counter in front of her. "C'mon."

She led them to a booth in the back corner, farthest from the front door. Kim placed a menu in front of Alissa, then looked at Danny. "You want one, too?"

"You know what I'm going to order," Danny said with a smile. Turning to Alissa, he explained, "I always get the same thing. It's become a joke."

"Corn chowder and a crab cake sandwich," Kim said. "Every single time!"

"I know every restaurant in Maryland says their crab cakes are the best, but these really are," Danny declared.

"Okay, you've sold me," Alissa said.

"Great." Kim made a note on her order pad. "And to drink?"

Alissa gave Danny a questioning look. If this was

a just-friends get-together, she should ask for iced tea or lemonade. Ordering alcohol might send the wrong message.

"I'll have a beer," Danny said. "How about you?"

"Sounds good," Alissa said.

The setting may have been different, but Danny and Alissa's conversation soon fell into its usual pattern: how things were progressing at the house, what the next project would be, which supplies needed to be ordered. Alissa had been on edge when they started out, but this easy back and forth calmed her jittery nerves. It was just Danny. They talked like this every day.

Still, the whole point of this dinner had been to find out more about him. It wasn't until they were well into their sandwiches that Alissa got up the courage to change the subject.

"We've been working together nearly every day for two months, but I know almost nothing about your personal life," she said lightly.

"That's because I don't have one," Danny said.

"C'mon," Alissa urged. "No girlfriend?"

Danny took a bite of his sandwich and swallowed before answering. "Not right now. I did, until last year."

"Yeah, me, too," Alissa said. "I mean, I had a boyfriend. For a long time."

"Ah. So that's why you escaped to the country."

"Not really," Alissa said. "Well—it's complicated."

"Isn't it always?" Danny said.

"Does she live around here?" Alissa asked. "Your ex?"

"No, she's in New York," Danny said. "Part of the life I left behind."

He made it sound so easy. Ditch the job, ditch the girl and move on. He sounded like a stereotypical guy, running away from any form of commitment. Alissa couldn't help feeling disappointed by his cavalier tone, shrugging off his past as though it meant nothing.

"Another beer?" Danny suggested.

"Sure."

When the second round of drinks arrived, Danny lifted his pint and clinked it against Alissa's glass. "To small towns," he toasted.

Alissa clinked her glass against his, then took a few sips. Danny had been wary about this evening, wondering how they'd relate to each other outside their usual routine. Seeing how beautiful she looked in that form-fitting dress had only made him more nervous. But gradually, as they ate, he felt himself loosen up, and Alissa had seemed at ease, too. Now, though, she put down her beer and swirled a couple of French fries aimlessly through a shallow pool of ketchup on her plate. Danny wondered if she was thinking about her boyfriend, the one she'd never mentioned before. He felt a sudden rush of jealousy.

"So, why did you two break up?" he asked casually.

"Lots of reasons," Alissa said. "We had completely different schedules, for one thing. Different priorities. The house was the final straw, though."

"How?"

"I fell in love with it, and he didn't."

Danny nodded as if that made sense.

By the time they finished dessert—slices of tart key lime pie—Alissa had drifted into a tipsy haze. She slipped in and out of attention as Danny talked about options for replacement windows. Even without listening to the exact words, it was reassuring to hear someone talk with such confidence. She watched his hands as he sketched ideas on a paper napkin.

"You tired?" Danny asked.

"What? Why?" Alissa said.

"You look distracted," he said. "Hope I'm not boring you."

"No, not at all," Alissa said. "I'm relaxed, that's all."

"Maybe I've never seen you relaxed before."

Alissa smiled, wanting to say something about his effect on her. If only she could find the right words.

Danny leaned back in his seat and casually studied her. "So, was it worth it? Trekking out here?" he asked.

"Absolutely. The food was great."

Danny grinned as if he'd cooked it himself. "I'm glad you liked it. Now you have someplace to bring your friends when they visit."

"What visits? My friends all think I live in the middle of nowhere." She laughed to show she was joking, but it wasn't far from the truth. Constance was the only person from her old life in Baltimore who'd made the trip out to see her.

"Maybe you'll make friends around here," Danny said. "We're not all hicks."

"Of course not. I never thought you were." Alissa wondered how she'd given him that impression. Before she could ask, Danny was putting his napkin on the table and saying, "Ready to go?"

They stood up, and Danny walked to the cash register by the door, holding the check Kim had left on the table earlier. As he pulled out his wallet, Alissa reached toward him.

"Let me," she offered.

"It's all right," Danny said.

Alissa put her hand on his arm. "No, really. I'm the one who asked you to dinner…."

"It's no big deal," Danny insisted.

Yet another reason not to mix business and pleasure, Alissa thought. You end up fighting over the check.

"Why don't we split it?" she suggested.

Danny shrugged. "Okay, if that's what you want."

They barely spoke on the drive back to Alissa's house. She wasn't sure if it was a comfortable silence, or a sign they'd run out of things to say.

As they pulled up in her driveway, Alissa flashed him the bright smile she used to give clients after business meetings. "Thanks so much. It was great to get out."

"Yeah," Danny said. "Listen…" He paused, and Alissa tensed up. Would he have the nerve to make a move? Did she want him to?

"If you ever need to get out again, give me a call, okay? I know it's hard to start out somewhere new. I'd be happy to introduce you around, if you like."

Danny's hand lay on the seat next to her. It would be so easy to touch him. A friendly gesture, nothing more. If she had sensed some flicker of movement, if Danny had so much as leaned in her direction, she would have reached for him. But he held back, letting Alissa know with his eyes that the first move would have to be hers.

Alissa turned away and picked up her purse. "See you tomorrow?"

"Right," he said. "I'll get started on the kitchen floor."

How easily he slipped back to business. It was as if the romantic tension between them had been a mirage, a feeling conjured up out of loneliness.

Back in the house, Alissa felt strangely listless. The dinner had gone as smoothly as she could have hoped, with good food and easy conversation. But the night had ended on an awkward note that bothered her. She knew, in the moment, she'd wanted to kiss Danny. Resisting that impulse had been a smart decision. Getting involved with someone who worked for her would be disastrous. But she couldn't help wondering what would have happened. Would he have come inside with her? How far would things have gone?

She turned on the TV in the living room and flipped aimlessly through the channels, too distracted to concentrate. She stared at the design magazines piled on the coffee table, unable to summon the energy to open them. Finally, she picked up the phone. She'd told Constance about her dinner plans earlier that day, and her friend had insisted she check in afterward.

"Hey," Alissa said when Constance picked up the phone. "Ready for the play-by-play of my nondate?"

"Tell me every scandalous detail," Constance said.

"Nothing scandalous, I'm afraid. We had dinner. Danny was a perfect gentleman."

"Oh." Constance sounded as disappointed as Alissa felt. "I was sure he'd put the moves on you. Or vice versa. How could you keep your hands off him?"

Alissa laughed. "I managed to resist temptation. It would make everything way too complicated."

Constance sighed. "You're right. I guess I wanted to live vicariously. You know, spice up my dull routine."

"Oh, please," Alissa scoffed. "You get out more than I do. Didn't you say you were going to the theater this week?"

"Yeah, last night." Constance hesitated before continuing. "I wasn't sure whether to bring this up, but—"

"What happened? Now you have to spill it," Alissa said, eager to deflect the attention away from herself.

"The play was awful," Constance said. "Much too long, and filled with pretentious overacting. Colin and I were walking around the lobby during intermission, trying to decide if we should skip the second half, and guess who we ran into. Brad."

This was a surprise. Going to the theater was one of the many things Alissa and Brad had fought about; Alissa had bought season tickets one year, and Brad had refused to go with her, calling it a waste of money.

"He was there with a woman," Constance continued. "Almost a girl, really. Young, petite. Pretty in a blank sort of way, but not beautiful, if that helps. We said hi, and stood there awkwardly, and I figured he'd be relieved if Colin and I went off to get a drink. It's not like we have anything to say to each other, right?

"But here's the weird part. Brad started asking about you—right there in front of his date. He wanted to know how you were doing, and if I'd seen you recently. It was more than the polite way you ask about someone you know in common—it was like he really wanted to know."

Brad. *Part of the life I left behind,* Alissa thought, remembering Danny's description of his ex-girlfriend.

"I wasn't even going to tell you," Constance said. "You and Brad are done, so why go over old ground again?"

"Yeah."

"You *are* over Brad, aren't you?" Constance asked.

"Of course." On some level, Alissa knew she was. Days went by when she didn't think of him. But questions about their relationship remained, ignored but not forgotten. A lingering unease about how things had ended.

"I'm not saying you should call him," Constance said. "It's probably better if you don't."

But Alissa knew she would. Sorting out her real feelings for Danny would be impossible if she didn't find closure with Brad first. Alissa thought of Evelyn Brewster, married in her early twenties. What if Alissa had married Brad at that age, when she didn't know any better? Her life might have been simpler, but she didn't think she would have been happier.

Had Evelyn ever lain awake at night, replaying conversations in her head, confused by her feelings? Maybe. But Charles Brewster was a great catch: rich, handsome and admired. There was no reason for Evelyn to have mixed feelings about him. Whereas Danny's good looks and easy charm had to be measured against his lack of ambition, his mysterious rootlessness. When it came to long-term prospects, Charles Brewster looked like a much better bet than Danny Pierce. Evelyn could never have known what it felt like to fall for the wrong man.

CHAPTER TWELVE

"AUNT EVELYN, what's wrong?"

Evelyn looked up from the dominoes stacked in front of her. Beatrice sat across the table, her eyes narrowed with concern. Evelyn might no longer be Beatrice's governess, but she still felt protective of her niece. She'd watched Lavinia and Alma dampen the girl's spirits as they attempted to transform her into an obedient young lady. Evelyn tried to counteract their efforts by spending time with Beatrice every week, time when Beatrice was allowed to have fun rather than sit dutifully like a miniature version of her mother. Usually, the visits were good for Evelyn, too. But today, she was too distracted to concentrate on their game.

"Sorry, love. I'm a bit tired," she said, forcing a smile.

"Why?"

"I had trouble sleeping last night."

"What's this about not sleeping?" a hearty voice boomed from behind her. Evelyn turned to see Winslow plodding across the room. Winslow never appeared to be in a hurry, or worried, or upset. For him, life was easy.

"Aunt Evelyn says she can't sleep!" Beatrice announced.

"That's not what I meant…" Evelyn insisted, shaking her head to quiet the child.

"Really?" Winslow asked, mystified by the concept of insomnia. "You need to rest a full eight hours each night. Nine, ideally. No reason to follow that 'early to rise' nonsense."

Not for him. Winslow didn't have to get up at dawn and work until nightfall to earn a living, as Evelyn's mother and so many others in Oak Hill did. He could roll out of bed at ten o'clock and enjoy a leisurely breakfast before shuffling papers for a few hours. Winslow had an official title at Brewster Shipping, but he didn't seem to spend much time at the Baltimore office. No doubt that was because Charles insisted on doing everything himself.

"Look, Daddy!" Beatrice said. "Her eyes are red!"

"Hush!" Evelyn admonished.

"Hope you're not ill," Winslow said. "One of the housemaids was sneezing this morning. It was quite distracting."

"I feel perfectly well, thank you. Beatrice, take your turn."

Evelyn turned her back to Winslow, hoping to discourage further conversation. But something in her tone had evidently piqued his interest.

"Evelyn?" She looked around to see Winslow staring at her with concern. "Are you sure you're all right?"

Caught off guard, Evelyn felt her eyes fill with tears. In the days following her conversation with Will, she'd braced herself to talk to Charles, but he hadn't been home all week. The constant uncertainty had sapped her strength.

"I'm tired, that's all," she said, blinking to catch the tears before they could fall.

"Yes, I imagine you would be," Winslow said. Their eyes met in a moment of understanding. He had sat through the Sunday dinners, watching Charles's treatment of her steadily deteriorate. By now, all of Baltimore must know that her marriage was troubled. Evelyn had assumed the family would unite against her, but perhaps she had an ally after all. Winslow would never openly side against Alma, but knowing he sympathized helped.

"Aunt Evelyn!" Beatrice demanded. "I put down my piece! It's your turn."

"You're right," Evelyn said. "Winslow—" She searched for something appropriate to say. "Thank you for your concern."

He smiled and gave a brief nod. "On with your game, girls."

Evelyn knew she would be ostracized if she divorced Charles, but Winslow had given her hope that she might not be shunned completely. He might even allow her to see Beatrice occasionally. Losing this bright, cheerful girl—whom she now thought of as her own flesh and blood—would be the most painful part of leaving the Brewster family.

THAT EVENING, as Evelyn sat down to another dinner alone in the vast dining room, she was startled by a commotion at the front door. She stood to investigate, but had only taken a few steps when Peggy rushed into the room.

"It's Mr. Brewster, ma'am," she announced. "He's

gone upstairs to change for dinner, and he says he'll join you momentarily. I must tell Mrs. Gower!" She dashed off toward the kitchen.

Evelyn's heart began to pound. How typical of Charles to give her no notice of his plans. He dined at home so rarely now that she had grown accustomed to eating by herself. She followed Peggy to the kitchen and saw Mrs. Gower relighting the stove. Peggy was frantically polishing a silver fork and knife.

"Do you have enough food?" Evelyn asked.

"I always make extra, just in case," Mrs. Gower said. "I'll heat this up a moment and have Peggy bring it in."

Evelyn returned to the table. She placed her napkin on her lap and smoothed out the creases, her hands moving over the linen as if they could calm her racing heart. Her appetite had disappeared.

"Darling." Charles walked into the room toward her, pressing a kiss to her forehead before taking his seat. The casual affection of the gesture startled her. "Sorry to interrupt your meal."

"Not at all," Evelyn said. Before she could say more, Peggy walked in with a plate of food, moving so unsteadily that Evelyn feared she would drop the whole thing. She placed it with a thump in front of Charles.

"Will that be all, sir?" Peggy asked.

"A bottle of wine," Charles said. "Red, don't you think, Evelyn?"

"Whichever you prefer."

"Red, then."

Peggy nodded and dashed back toward the kitchen. Evelyn half expected to hear the crash of a broken bottle in the distance.

"Not much of a welcome," Charles said with a smile. "I expected to be greeted at the door with an embrace from my devoted wife."

Evelyn stared at him, uncertain how to respond. Charles laughed at her confusion.

"Doesn't it amuse you?" he asked. "Putting on a pretense of a loving marriage for the staff? Ah—here's the wine!"

Peggy struggled to uncork the bottle. After a few tense moments, Charles stood up and took the bottle from her hand. "Allow me." He popped the cork and nodded to the young maid.

Peggy was clearly relieved by her dismissal. No doubt she and Mrs. Gower would be listening at the door throughout the meal. Evelyn wondered if Charles would continue the doting-husband charade for their benefit.

Charles poured a glass of wine for himself, then held the bottle out to Evelyn. She shook her head. She needed to think clearly tonight.

"So," Charles began, slicing his meat with forceful strokes, "I thought it time we had a talk."

"I agree."

"It must be clear to you—as it is to me—that our situation is untenable."

Was Charles about to ask her for a divorce? Evelyn hadn't dared to hope it would be this easy.

"I blame myself," he continued. "I should have been frank with you from the beginning. I thought, given your obvious intelligence, that certain aspects of our marriage would be understood. I overlooked your sheltered upbringing." He raised his hand as Evelyn started to protest. "Yes, yes, you attended college and helped support your family by working in that dreadful shop. I didn't say you had an easy life. But it was a sheltered one. You weren't exposed to society. And you had a rather romantic idea of what marriage entailed."

He paused to take a bite of food and chew leisurely. Evelyn clutched her napkin under the table.

"You must understand that I never intended to be faithful to you," Charles stated. "I'm simply not made for fidelity, my dear. I was entranced by you, of course. I even imagined I was in love with you for a while. Keeping me at a distance was a brilliant maneuver on your part. Allowing me only a kiss here and there kept me hungry for more.

"I could have married anyone, as my mother never tires of telling me. But so many of the debutantes I met in New York and Philadelphia could talk of nothing other than clothes and society gossip. The way you spoke up for yourself was refreshing. I could tolerate a silly mistress—one doesn't take a mistress for the conversation—but I would have to marry someone with wit and intelligence.

"I didn't want a clingy wife, either. I'm not one to sit quietly by the fire at home. So many of the women I met viewed their suitors as substitutes for their fathers—men who would indulge their every whim and drown them in compliments. I wanted a woman who wouldn't depend on me to meet every need."

"And these are the reasons you lowered yourself to marry me?" Evelyn couldn't meet his eyes.

"Certainly, I would have met with far less resistance from my family had I married someone of my own class." Charles gulped down the remainder of his wine and refilled the glass. "I met a few suitable young women who appeared both intelligent and independent. But a woman from a powerful family would have presented another sort of difficulty. She might have expected behavior of which I am incapable."

"Such as fidelity?" Evelyn asked bitterly.

"I need to live my life as I please," Charles said. "The last thing I wanted was a father-in-law who would lecture me about my behavior over cigars after dinner."

"And I had no father. No one to defend my reputation."

"Enough!" Charles snapped. "My decision wasn't completely coldhearted. You forget what passion you inspired in me. I greatly anticipated our wedding night."

Evelyn remembered the strength of his hands a few weeks before, as he slapped her face and forced himself upon her. She couldn't think of a time when he had touched her body tenderly.

"I've given you a good life, haven't I?" Charles said. He lifted up one hand, indicating the dining room's expensive French wallpaper and crystal chandelier. "You want for nothing."

"Nothing but my husband's affection," Evelyn said quietly.

Charles smiled. "Well said. You have not lost your tart tongue after all." His cheeks were ruddy, and Evelyn noticed that his glass was empty again. He paused to fill it, then raised the goblet in her direction.

"I propose a toast. To a new beginning."

This must be it. He was ready to suggest a separation.

"I would like to correct my earlier oversight and make clear my expectations for this marriage," Charles went on. "From this day forward I will treat you as my wife in public and accompany you to events as necessary. You will continue to enjoy all the benefits of the Brewster name and fortune. You will live in this house, and I will increase your allowance so you may buy gowns in New York, if you please. I will even offer a settlement to your mother—it's only right that I support my own mother-in-law."

Evelyn's heart sank. Charles wasn't offering escape. He was setting the terms of her imprisonment.

"In exchange, I will conduct my private life as I wish." Charles drained his wine glass yet again. "When I come home, I expect to be treated as a husband, with all the rights that implies. If you are willing to be accommodating, perhaps I will feel inclined to produce that heir my mother is so anxious for."

Charles would keep humiliating her, and he expected her to be grateful. The sting of disappointment overrode Evelyn's fear.

"May I make another suggestion?" she asked. Charles poured the last of the wine into his glass.

"Surely, this is no way to conduct a marriage." Evelyn spoke carefully, trying to present her case in a way that would show the benefit to him. "Clearly, I am not suited to this sort of life. If you were free of me, able to do as you pleased…"

"How is that possible?"

"A divorce," Evelyn said.

For a moment, she thought it might work. "It would be best for both of us. I would take the blame, and I wouldn't ask for any financial support…."

"Financial support!" Charles shouted. Evelyn shrank back in her chair from the force of his anger.

"You want to ruin my reputation and my family's good name, yet I'm supposed to be grateful that you aren't asking for financial support? Have you gone mad?"

"Surely it would be preferable to this," Evelyn said.

"Perhaps when you're an O'Keefe you can speak lightly of such things. Do you have any idea what repercussions a divorce would have for me? I'd be laughed at behind my back. Subjected to the most insulting gossip. My mother and sister would be humiliated. How dare you suggest such a thing!"

He slammed his empty wineglass on the table. Evelyn kept her eyes on her plate. The sight of the cold, congealed fat around the roast beef brought on a wave of nausea.

"I can't imagine…" Charles began, then stopped suddenly. He grabbed Evelyn's arm. "Is there another reason?" The rage in his eyes made her cringe, but he held her firmly in place. "Someone else?"

In her terror, there was only one possible response. "No," she said. "Of course not."

He released her with a shove. "No, you would never be that stupid." Charles was incapable of seeing the world through anyone else's eyes. He expected Evelyn to turn a blind eye to his affairs, but he would never tolerate infidelity from her.

"There will be no more talk of divorce," Charles said. "I'd hoped we could settle this in a friendly manner. Instead, you insult me."

Evelyn searched for a way to calm him. Would he believe her if she apologized and pretended to agree with him? She could manage to be a dutiful wife for one evening.

"It's been a difficult evening," she said, picking up her napkin and placing it on the table. "Tomorrow, perhaps, we can find a solution that suits us both."

She stood up and quickly walked past Charles, hoping he would stay behind. The thought of what he might do made her light-headed with fear. As she crossed the foyer toward the stairs, she heard him approaching behind her.

"That's all?" he asked, grasping her shoulder and forcing her around to look at him. Evelyn saw his red cheeks, his cold eyes. At that moment, she hated him.

"I'm exhausted." She could barely keep her voice level. She wriggled out of his grip and turned to walk up the stairs. She kept her steps slow and steady, afraid of provoking him by moving too fast.

"A husband has rights," he said. She felt his breath on the back of her neck as he followed her upstairs.

She reached the top of the staircase. The door to the bedroom was only a few feet away. "You're drunk," she said, turning to face him. "Surely there's another woman whose bed you would share tonight?"

"Ah, that's the spitfire I married!" He laughed.

Evelyn inched backward, watching Charles as she would a wild dog with its teeth bared.

"Seeing you angry sparks something in me." Charles put his hand out for her, but she was just beyond his reach. "You wouldn't deny me, would you, wife?"

Evelyn looked down demurely. "Perhaps if you gave me a moment alone, to prepare myself."

"What surprises do you have in store?" His words were slurred.

Evelyn spun around and dashed through the doorway to her bedroom. She slammed the door closed with one hand and locked it. Charles shook the handle outside.

"What are you doing?" he shouted.

"You're drunk!" Evelyn shouted back. "Leave me be!"

There was a sudden crash as Charles flung himself against the door. "This is my house!" he bellowed. "You can't lock me out!"

Evelyn backed away from the door as it shuddered under Charles's assault. What would he do to her if he broke in? She crouched on the floor next to the bed, wrapping her hands around her legs to stop the shivers that rippled through her body. Even if he did get in, Mrs. Gower and Peggy were downstairs. They couldn't help but hear this. They would help her get away if he tried to hurt her.

Or would they? Charles—and, by extension, Alma—paid their wages. They might feel sorry for Evelyn, but they would never take a stand against the Brewsters.

Then, suddenly, there was silence. Evelyn waited a few minutes, wondering if Charles was trying to trick her. She crept over to the door and pressed her ear against the wood. She heard footsteps stomping down the hallway toward Charles's room. A little while later, the steps passed her door again and clattered down the stairs. The front door slammed behind him.

He was gone. Evelyn slid into her bed, fully clothed, and gathered the blankets over her shoulders. She huddled there, terrified, remembering the rage in Charles's eyes when he'd accused her of being unfaith-

ful. He would never agree to a divorce. And he must
never find out about her love for Will. He was capable
of killing them both.

CHAPTER THIRTEEN

ALISSA SPOTTED Brad immediately, sitting at the bar of the tapas lounge he'd suggested in downtown Baltimore. The time apart had revived him. He looked healthier and happier than he had during the months their relationship had crumbled. His suit was tailored to highlight his muscular frame, and his skin had the ruddy tone that came with weekend golf rounds and after-work pickup basketball games. He flashed Alissa the wide smile he used to dazzle her with when they'd started dating.

Alissa had forgotten how handsome Brad could be when he made an effort. Over their years of dating, his face had become so familiar that she'd no longer noticed. After seeing him in every possible mood—from gleefully enthusiastic to hungover and irritable—she'd taken for granted the qualities that had first attracted her to him. His dark, penetrating eyes. The well-defined shoulders. Alissa was surprised to discover that even after their painful history, she could still admire Brad on a physical level.

"Alissa!" he exclaimed, standing up to give her a hug. "I ordered a pitcher of sangria, okay?"

Alissa nodded as Brad pulled out a tall metal bar chair for her to sit on. They'd never eaten here before, but he'd known what she would order. He could probably pick her favorite dishes off the menu, too.

"It's great to see you," he said.

"You, too," Alissa said. She wasn't sure if she meant it.

Alissa had been curious when Constance mentioned that Brad had been asking about her. At the time, it had seemed perfectly reasonable to call him and check in. When he invited her to dinner, she told herself that having one final conversation was the only way to put the relationship behind her at last. But as Alissa drove to the city that night, she wondered if what she really wanted was to test herself. See if any lingering feelings remained. Standing here, next to Brad, she felt the old attraction flicker. She noticed another woman at the bar eye him admiringly and was disturbed by her pang of jealousy.

Despite her nerves and the distracting salsa music blaring through the ceiling speakers, their conversation unfolded smoothly enough after they ordered. That was mostly due to Brad, who'd always been able to make small talk even in the most awkward circumstances.

They covered the expected topics: work, people they knew in common, Alissa's progress on the house.

Diners continued to file through the door behind them, and the restaurant was soon packed. Once, Alissa might have found this place exciting, with its garishly colorful murals and cacophony of voices and clattering plates. But after the quiet of Oak Hill, it was almost overwhelming.

"So, are you seeing anyone?" Alissa asked, trying to feign indifference, looking at her plate of marinated olives rather than Brad.

Brad laughed. "I wondered how long it would take you to ask!"

"Why?"

"I know Constance told you she saw me with a woman. You're curious. Admit it!"

Alissa smiled. "All right. I'm curious."

"It's not what you think. Erica and I work together. She had an extra ticket, I was bored, so I went with her. I guess it might've been a date, sort of, but there was no spark."

Alissa tried to keep her expression impassive, but she felt relieved. Not because she was still interested in Brad—she knew that now—but because she didn't want him to move on before she did. It wouldn't seem fair, somehow.

"How about you?" Brad asked.

Alissa shook her head. "Oak Hill isn't exactly crawling with single guys. Besides, all I do is work."

"I figured." Brad held up the sangria pitcher and offered to pour her another glass.

Alissa shook her head. "I've got to drive home."

"Not necessarily." Brad shot her a devious look.

Alissa gazed at him, acknowledging the invitation in his eyes. Once, that look would have made her heart pound. She was tempted for a brief moment, seeing Brad in this sultry setting, as he turned the full force of his attention on her. But changing her life had taken all her strength and nerve. Slipping off to Brad's apartment would only send her spiraling backward.

"I'd better not," she said.

"I get it." Brad smiled as if he'd been joking all along. "You've got to get up early to strip floors."

"Something like that."

"You sure you're not pushing yourself too hard? No one can believe you're renovating that huge place by yourself."

Alissa flashed to an image of Danny working in the kitchen. Sitting on the front porch eating a sandwich, laughing when she pointed out the plaster in his hair.

"I've got some help," she said.

"Weren't you going to start your own design firm? What happened with that?"

"I'm focusing on the house right now," Alissa said defensively. For years, she'd talked about leaving her job and starting over. Now that she'd finally made the leap, what did she have to show for it? She had almost no career left, very little money and no social life. Just the house.

"I knew that place would wear you down," Brad said.

"You never liked it," Alissa said.

"I didn't see what the big deal was. It put some kind of spell on you."

He would never understand. Neither would most of the people she'd thought of as friends. Only Danny knew what the Brewster house meant to her. How important it was to preserve it. Like Alissa, he felt the house deserved the work they put into it, no matter how exhausting or time-consuming.

It would be easy to slip back into old habits, to let Brad take the lead and point out her mistakes. But she was a different person now. Yes, it was fun being in a hip restaurant for a night, but she no longer felt as if she belonged in this world. She'd found her home. And Brad had no place there.

"You and me—it didn't have anything to do with the house," Alissa said. "We would've broken up even if I hadn't bought it. You know that, right?"

Brad scanned the room, as if checking out his other prospects, before setting on Alissa.

"Yeah," he finally agreed. "Just so you know, I did try to make it work."

"Me, too." Alissa reached across the table and gave his hand a quick squeeze. The feel of his fingers under hers was comfortable, nothing more. There was none of the electricity she felt with Danny.

"Maybe you should give Erica another try," she suggested. "She must have some good points if she convinced you to go to the theater."

They laughed together, a shared joke between old friends. Alissa could imagine a future—faintly, as if squinting at a far-off, blurry photograph—when she and Brad could talk occasionally, happy for each other as they each built new lives. When the thought of him with another woman had lost its sting. They weren't quite there yet. But one day they might be.

Alissa drove home with the windows down, not caring that the wind tangled her hair. She turned up the dance music on the local Top 40 radio station and bobbed her head to the music. She felt liberated. A tiny but persistent thread had connected her to her old life, subtly tugging at her whenever she tried to move forward. Now the thread had been cut. There were no more lingering doubts.

As Alissa pulled into her driveway, she was surprised to see Danny's truck parked out front. Her headlights illuminated his lean figure standing in the back, reaching into the flatbed. Returning to an empty house had never bothered her, but she was surprisingly relieved to see him.

Alissa stopped her car and stepped outside. "Hey there!"

"Hi. Sorry to bother you. I was at my friend Ed's house, and he had these extra tarps, so I thought I'd drop them off since it was on the way home. I'll be out of your hair in a minute."

"Sure." Alissa started to climb the front steps, then turned back. "You want to come in? I was going to make some tea."

"Sounds good. Thanks," Danny said.

Alissa wasn't nervous or doubtful as she walked to the kitchen and put the kettle on the stove. She searched the plastic storage cart she used for dishes now that the old cabinets had been torn off and found two mugs, both chipped but acceptable. When Danny came in, it felt right to turn to smile, to tilt her head up, without a word, and watch him lean down toward her. To feel him take her face in his hands and kiss her.

As their lips met, Alissa's arms reached around Danny's waist, and he pulled her close. He kissed her gently, waiting for her to set the tone. They stood together, their lips expressing what they had been too afraid to say, as the kettle hissed, forgotten, in the background.

CHAPTER FOURTEEN

EVELYN WOKE to someone knocking on her bedroom door. She pulled the blanket tightly around her as if it could block out the force of Charles's anger.

"Ma'am?" Not Charles. Peggy.

"Just a minute." Evelyn pulled herself out from under the covers and unlocked the door.

"Sorry to wake you, only it's your usual breakfast time...."

"No, no, it's all right," Evelyn said, ushering her in.

Peggy usually chattered aimlessly as she brought in the breakfast tray, but this morning she was uncharacteristically silent. She dropped the tray on the bedside table with a loud clatter and avoided looking directly at Evelyn. Evelyn realized she was still wearing her clothes from the night before, when she had run into the bedroom and locked the door against Charles's onslaught. No doubt Peggy would be describing her disheveled outfit and matted hair—not to mention the locked door—to the rest of the staff as soon as she got downstairs.

"I was so tired last night," Evelyn said, forcing a smile. "I didn't even bother to change."

"Do you need anything else, Mrs. Brewster?" Peggy asked.

"No. Oh—actually, there is one thing. Is Mr. Brewster breakfasting downstairs?"

Peggy shook her head. "No, ma'am. Mrs. Trimble told me Mr. Brewster woke her husband late last night and had him saddle up one of the horses. He said he'd be gone a few days."

"Thank you, Peggy. That's all for now."

She was safe. Charles would throw himself into his work and distract himself with other women until he decided what to do with her. In the meantime, she could plan her next move.

Evelyn remembered the sound of his fists beating against her door. What would he do the next time? She considered packing a suitcase and running to the train station. Some of her friends from college lived in Philadelphia. Surely they would let her stay if she appeared at their door, desperate for help. Charles would never think to look for her there.

But that would mean leaving Will. She could write to him once she was safely away, but any letter sent to the main house would be easily intercepted by Alma. No, she must tell Will first, in person. Before she made her escape, she had to make sure he was ready to leave everything behind for her.

EVELYN CONTINUED with her normal routine in the following days. She had her mother for lunch that afternoon, as she did every Friday, and met with Mrs. Trimble to discuss menus and shopping lists for the following week. All the while, she worried Charles would come back for Alma's Sunday dinner. She left an urgent note for Will under the garden bench, and although it was gone by Saturday morning, there was no reply.

Luckily, Beatrice provided some distraction. Evelyn had invited her niece over for the day, and Beatrice was clearly thrilled.

"Can we have a tea party?" Beatrice begged as she ran into Evelyn's outstretched arms.

"What a lovely idea."

Beatrice threw her head backward, gazing up at the glittering chandelier above. "Can I stay here when I'm grown up?" she asked.

Evelyn looked around the grand foyer. She loved this house. But if staying here meant living with Charles, she would gladly give it up.

"We can live together!" Beatrice exclaimed. "Wouldn't that be fun?"

Evelyn pressed her face to the girl's shoulder. She wanted to tell her how much she loved her. How she'd been a bright spot in a very dark, difficult time. But she could give no hint of her plans in case Alma got wind of it. Already, her heart ached at the thought of Beatrice's bewilderment when she found out her aunt had disappeared without a word.

The following day brought the event Evelyn had dreaded: dinner at Alma's. Although Charles did not return home earlier in the day, Evelyn knew there was a chance he would go straight to his mother's house. When she entered Alma's parlor in the late afternoon, she saw only Lavinia's family and Will. She smiled with relief, then caught sight of her mother-in-law's disapproving frown.

"Evelyn," Alma said, nodding in her usual brusque fashion.

"Good evening, Alma. Have you heard from Charles? Will he be joining us?" Evelyn asked.

Alma stared at her disapprovingly. "Do you not even know where your own husband is?" she asked. "He's in Washington seeing to some business matters. Although I don't see what could be so very urgent on a Sunday."

"Oh." How typical of Charles to inform Alma of his plans but leave his wife in the dark. Perhaps it was a strategy to keep her always on edge.

"Aunt Evelyn!" Beatrice said happily, running toward her. "Grandmother says I can sit next to you!"

"Wonderful," Evelyn said. Evelyn's place at the dinner table had been the same every week since her marriage, between Charles and Lavinia. Today, however, she found herself seated between Beatrice and Will.

"Evelyn, you're looking well," Will said casually as they sat down. He could have been addressing a distant cousin.

"Thank you," Evelyn said. Seeing him here, so close, filled her with longing. It would be so easy to reach under the table and brush her fingers against his. But she didn't dare. Once she caught hold of him, she might never let go.

"I hear my brother is unable to join us this evening," Will said.

"Apparently, he is quite burdened with business obligations."

"A pity." Will's eyes twinkled, mocking his words.

"Yes, it's a shame," Evelyn agreed.

The dinner-table conversation followed the usual

progression. Alma commented disapprovingly on acquaintances and neighbors; Lavinia scolded Beatrice; Will attempted to lighten the mood with humor; and Winslow bored them all with stories about his childhood escapades. As Evelyn responded to Will's questions with exaggerated politeness, she grew increasingly desperate. She had to tell him she couldn't wait much longer to escape. But how?

Alma seemed determined to keep them apart. After dinner, when Will challenged Evelyn to a game of cards at a table in the back of the sitting room, Alma urged Lavinia and Winslow to join them. When Evelyn moved to the couch, Alma sat next to her. Finally, after the sun had long since set and everyone had drained their second cups of tea or coffee, Will offered to escort Evelyn home. Alma insisted she ride in Lavinia's carriage instead.

"Surely that would be most convenient for everyone," she said. "There's no need for Will to traipse around in this weather—it looks like rain."

As Evelyn descended the front steps behind Lavinia and Winslow, she could only turn and give Will a brief, pleading glance. Perhaps he would leave a letter for her tonight.

Evelyn returned to an empty house. Usually, she looked forward to these quiet Sunday evenings alone, free from the servants' constant surveillance. Gloomy Mrs. Trimble and her silent husband spent the weekends in their cottage on the edge of the property; Peggy and Mrs. Gower took advantage of their evening off to stay with relatives in town, returning to work Monday morning. In the early weeks of their marriage, Evelyn and Charles would arrive home after dinner at Alma's and go their separate ways: Charles retreating to his office while Evelyn sat in the conservatory, curled up with a book. After being surrounded by other people all day, such solitude was liberating.

But tonight, for the first time, the empty house frightened her. Peggy had forgotten to light the lamps before she left, so Evelyn arrived to find the house plunged in darkness. She felt her way down the hall to the kitchen, where she found matches and a candle. Moving back toward the front of the house, she heard what sounded like breaking glass. Startled, she peered into the parlor. She heard the tinkling sound again, but all the windows here were intact. Through the window, she saw sleet beating down outside. That must have been the sound she heard. Miserable weather to complement her miserable mood.

She lit a lamp on a side table, then paused. Was it worth lighting up the room just to sit here alone? Perhaps she should go upstairs. Light the fire in her bedroom and settle in bed with a book. Yet she found herself unwilling to move. The thought of climbing the stairs and walking along the hall with only a candle made her nervous. Could Charles have come back while she was at Alma's? Was he waiting for her in the bedroom, ready to surprise her? He knew the servants were gone, and he could do what he liked....

A floorboard creaked at the back of the house, and Evelyn froze. For a moment, she considered running upstairs and barricading herself in her room. No, that would be foolish. Charles wouldn't sneak up on her— he would confront her face-to-face. He enjoyed seeing her fear.

"Evelyn."

The whisper came from the far end of the parlor, near the conservatory. Staring into the darkness, she saw a figure approaching. Will. Her Will.

The force of her embrace made him catch his breath.

"So much for being discreet." He laughed, running his hands down her back.

"What are you doing here?" she demanded, her voice angry even as her body sagged with relief. "How did you get in?"

"I broke the lock in the conservatory," he said. "One of the many unsavory skills I learned in my youth. I'll tell you the story one day."

Evelyn clung to him, afraid to let go and be alone in the darkness again.

"I know it's awfully rude to turn up like this," Will said, "but I didn't want Peggy announcing me at the front door."

"The servants have Sunday off," Evelyn said. "There's no one here."

"So my trespassing was entirely unnecessary!" He laughed. "That would've saved me a very wet walk through your garden."

Evelyn looked down at his trousers and shoes, which were dripping water onto the floor. She ran her hands down his sleeves, which were also soaked, and felt the chill of his fingers.

"You must be freezing," she said. "Come—I'll get some towels."

She led him down the hall to the kitchen. She found Mrs. Gower's stack of white dish towels on a shelf and started patting at Will's clothes.

"Can't say I feel much warmer," Will said.

"You need dry clothes," Evelyn said. "I could get you something of Charles's."

Will looked at her doubtfully.

"It's better than catching the flu," she insisted. "Why don't you light a fire in the parlor, and I'll be right back."

Upstairs, Evelyn's candle created a small halo of light in the darkened hallway. She entered Charles's room. The space offered no clues about its occupant— no pictures on the wall, no cuff links on the nightstand. It still looked like the sparsely decorated guest bedroom it had once been. Evelyn rifled through the clothes in the armoire. She pulled out a pair of tweed trousers and a wool shirt she'd never seen him wear. Tonight, she wanted no reminders of her husband.

She left the room, her pace quicker now as she returned to Will. As she opened the door to the parlor, she stopped at the sight before her. Will sat on the floor in front of the fireplace, his shirt unbuttoned and hanging off his shoulders. He was leaning toward the fire, and the heat of the flames flushed his face.

"Sorry," he said, looking up at her. "I was so cold."

Evelyn remained in the doorway. She wanted to hold on to this image. The man she loved, waiting for her, caught in a moment when anything seemed possible.

"Come." He spoke gently, but the word had the force of a command. Evelyn walked toward him, Charles's clothes dropping from her arms as Will pulled her down next to him. She moved her hands along his shoulders and down his back, pushing aside his drenched shirt. She pressed herself against him, trying to warm him with her touch.

"Evelyn, whatever happens," he whispered, "don't ever doubt that I love you."

"How could I?" she said. And it was true. Here, now, with Will, all her fears evaporated. Of course they would be together. When it felt so right to be with him, how could she be anywhere else?

They lay together in the glow of the fire. When Will reached tentatively for her blouse, she helped him undo the tiny mother-of-pearl buttons, laughing as their fingers tangled. His kisses made her light-headed. He waited for her approval before touching her in places Charles never had. He was careful, so careful and patient. She found herself responding to him in ways she never thought possible. Slowly, easily, their clothes slipped aside. Evelyn felt Will's breath on her neck, ragged and desperate, and she clung to him, pressing her lips to his lean shoulders and arms. As they came together, she was overtaken by the waves of pleasure that blazed through her body. In Will's arms, she felt complete.

Afterward, Evelyn reached for her blouse and skirt.

"Are you cold?" Will asked.

"No, not really."

"Then let me look at you."

She blushed, and Will folded her into his embrace. The firelight flickered over their bodies as they lay entwined. She could have drifted off to sleep. Already this evening had taken on the hazy unreality of a dream.

Then Evelyn caught sight of Charles's shirt lying on the floor. A reminder of the life she had tried so hard to escape for one night.

"Will, we need to talk."

"Yes." His voice was a lazy drawl.

"Charles will never agree to a divorce. He suspected I might be leaving him for someone else—I denied it, of course—and his anger was terrifying. If he were to walk in now and see us..." Evelyn's voice rose with panic.

"Hush," Will said, trailing his fingers along her arm. "He's hours away, in Washington. Spending his inheritance on women of ill-repute, I'd hazard. Or drinking himself into an early grave."

"But he could come back tomorrow. I can't be alone with him. I'm so afraid. I have to leave, no matter how it makes me look, but I don't know where, or how—"

"Calm down," Will urged. "I've thought of a plan."

"You have?"

"One way or another, your marriage has to end. You've said you don't give a care about your reputation, and mine is already ruined. A divorce is the only solution."

"I told you, Charles will fight it."

"Of course he will, at first. But I've spoken to some lawyers—all very discreet, don't worry. If life were fair, you would be granted a divorce on grounds of adultery. You and I know Charles is guilty, but proving it would be another matter."

"We never could," Evelyn said. "No one would dare speak against him."

"And you would subject yourself to a humiliating legal battle with very little hope of winning. But there is another possibility. Abandonment."

"What would I have to do?"

"Leave. Disappear. After a certain amount of time has passed, you could write to Charles and ask for a divorce. It could take years, I'm afraid, but by then, he'll be anxious to be rid of you. You'll accept blame for leaving the marriage, he can emerge as the innocent victim, and some unlucky young fortune hunter can become the next Mrs. Brewster."

"Do you think it could work?"

"If you have the patience. And the strength."

"It will take more than strength," Evelyn said. "I don't have the money to disappear for a month, let alone years. I've saved all I can, but it's not nearly enough."

"Money is the least of your worries," Will said. "Didn't I tell you I would find a solution? I've been putting money aside for years. A form of insurance, as I'm quite sure none of the Brewster fortune will be coming my way in Mother's will. I wasted a fair amount on wine and motorcars—something I deeply regret now—but I can afford to buy train tickets. And food, for a time at least. Enough to leave."

"But that money is yours," Evelyn protested.

Will held her tighter. "Don't you see? I'm using the money to get what I want most in the world—you. If I have to spend every penny to free you from Charles, it will be worth it."

"You'll come with me?"

"There's nowhere I would rather be."

Evelyn smiled with relief. "Then we'll go. Tonight, even. It won't take long for me to pack a bag...."

"I admire your enthusiasm." Will smiled. "But we wouldn't get far. No trains run at this time of night. You can wait until tomorrow, can't you?"

"But Charles—"

"When was the last time he rushed home to see you

during the day?" Will asked. "I doubt he'd be home before dinner, if then."

"I suppose," Evelyn said.

"Don't tell anyone about your plans, not even a hint," Will said. "Go through your day as usual, and I'll sort out the travel arrangements. I'll come for you in the afternoon, at the latest. Well before Charles would be expected home."

"If we disappear on the same day, the whole family will know you've gone with me."

"By then, it won't matter," Will said. "Let them be horrified. Although I admit, I would love to see Mother's face when she finds out!"

Evelyn laughed nervously at the thought of Alma's reaction. It would be the perfect comeuppance. After years spent denigrating others, Alma would finally be the subject of scandalous gossip.

"Where should we go?" she asked.

"I have an idea," Will said. "Are you willing to trust me?"

She nodded.

"Good. All you need to do is pack a bag. I hope you're not one of those women who insists on traveling with fourteen trunks of clothing."

"Apparently, I won't be requiring much clothing at all," Evelyn said with a smile.

"How promising," Will murmured. He reached for her, and soon they were distracted by the feel of each other's bodies.

"Come upstairs," Evelyn whispered. "So many nights, I've imagined you in my bed. If this is my last night here, I want you to spend it with me."

They climbed the stairs together, fueled by anticipation. All through that stormy night, they kissed and whispered plans for the future, as if imagining a new life could erase their fears for the day to come.

CHAPTER FIFTEEN

AS SHE AWOKE in her bedroom, Alissa flashed back to the previous night. Kissing Danny in the kitchen. Pulling away as the teakettle grew more insistent. Standing there, wondering what to do. Pour the tea as if nothing had happened? Or turn off the burner and drag Danny out of the kitchen, to the couch—or even upstairs?

She remembered the way Danny had watched her, his cautious smile an invitation. Paralyzed by indecision, she'd held back. If he'd taken one step toward her, reached out with his confident hands, he might have wiped away her doubts. But Danny would never push her for more than she was ready to give. She had to come for him this time.

His smile had faded in Alissa's silence. "I should go," he'd said.

"Oh."

His body had responded to her, she was sure of that, and he looked hurt as he turned away. Alissa realized, too late, that Danny had been hoping she'd protest, pull him back into her arms. By the time she figured it out, he was gone.

Alissa glanced at the clock on her bedside table. Danny would be showing up for work within the hour.

She pushed off the covers and made her way to the bathroom, catching her reflection in the mirror attached to the wall across the room. It was an unusual piece, almost as tall as she was and surrounded by an elaborate gilded frame. At first she'd found it charming, in a quirky sort of way, but now she was having second thoughts. She'd recently had to buy an armoire—lack of closet space being a major drawback of historic homes—and it came with a full-length mirror inside one of the doors. Maybe Danny could take this one down without doing too much damage to the plaster.

Danny. It was just as well she hadn't brought him up here last night. How would she have faced him this morning? How would they have moved from lovers to employer and employee in just a few hours? She thought back to the peaceful feeling that had enveloped her during the drive home from Baltimore. She knew with complete certainty that she had made the right decision about her life. When she saw Danny standing in the driveway, she'd simply followed her instincts. Kissing him had felt like the natural next step.

At least they hadn't gone too far. But there was no denying she'd led him on, then rejected him, and she felt terrible for toying with his feelings. She hoped he'd play it cool this morning. She couldn't afford to lose him—as a handyman, but even more as a friend.

Alissa was halfheartedly dusting the carved banister by the front door when Danny walked in.

"Feeling okay?" he asked.

"I guess," Alissa said warily.

"I thought I'd find you groaning in bed with the curtains pulled shut."

He was going to pass this off as a drunken mistake. Maybe the kiss hadn't affected him as much as she thought. Alissa forced a laugh as she followed his lead.

"Sangria. Guess I should be more careful."

"I'll keep the hammering to a minimum," Danny said. He strolled down the hall to the kitchen as if last night had never happened, which Alissa found both reassuring and infuriating.

By unspoken mutual agreement, they ate lunch separately, Danny in the kitchen and Alissa upstairs in her room. By midafternoon, Alissa had tired of the charade. If she and Danny were going to make any progress on the renovations, they could hardly do so from opposite ends of the house. So what if she kept thinking about that kiss, remembering the feel of his body pressed up against her? The sooner they got back to normal, the better.

She called down to him from the top of the stairs.

"Yeah?" He walked into the foyer, wiping sweat off his forehead with a rag he'd pulled from the waistband of his jeans.

"When you've got a minute, there's something I'd like you to do in my bedroom." As soon as she heard herself, she blushed. Last night had given even the simplest request new meaning.

"Really?" Danny asked with a broad smile and Alissa's face flushed deeper. "C'mon, I'm kidding," he said.

"Right, I know," Alissa said, stumbling over the words.

Danny took the stairs two at a time. When he reached the top, he leaned over, resting one arm on the railing so he could look Alissa in the eye.

"Can we get something straight?" he asked.

She nodded.

"You don't have to feel bad about what happened. It was late, you were a bit tipsy, I got caught up in the moment—it's no big deal."

But it was, Alissa realized. Although she'd tried to distract herself with paint samples and plastering, it hadn't worked.

"So," Alissa said, keeping her tone light, "I guess you make out with all your clients?"

"Actually, no." Danny looked at her seriously. "You're the first. But if you're not ready, or you've had second thoughts, that's cool. Just tell me so."

Alissa wanted to say the kiss didn't mean anything, that they should go back to being no more than casual friends. But she couldn't. Danny could be infuriatingly mysterious about his past, but he'd always been honest with her. If he really wanted to get things straight, she owed him no less than the truth.

"I'm not sure how I feel about last night," Alissa said. "I guess because I'm not sure how I feel about you."

"Oh." Danny's expression was neutral. He was waiting for her to reveal her hand before making his next move.

"I can't figure you out," Alissa said. "You have an MBA, you've traveled all over the world, but here you are, working as a small-town handyman. Don't you want something better?"

"Who's to say what's better?" Danny asked with a smile. Seeing that Alissa wasn't in the mood for joking, he sighed and ran both hands through his hair, as if clearing his head of all distractions.

"You want to know if I'm a screwup, right?"

Alissa began to protest, but Danny waved her off.

"Maybe I am," he said. "I've made more than my share of mistakes. Starting with going to business school and getting drawn into a competition that I never really wanted to win. You know, I only interviewed for that investment bank job to prove I could. I never thought I'd get it, and I sure as hell didn't realize what I was getting into when I accepted it. I ended up making an insane amount of money, found myself a flashy girlfriend and a cool apartment, but in the end the pressure wore me down. I had to walk away."

Alissa remembered their conversation at Jack's Place, when Danny had talked about leaving his life and his girlfriend behind. She'd assumed he wanted to play the field rather than be tied to one woman. Now she saw that Danny's search for freedom went even deeper. He didn't want a steady relationship or a steady job, or even a home of his own. He was content to live an aimless life, in the small town where he'd grown up. He was smart and kind, but utterly without ambition.

Strangely, Alissa found this realization liberating. She could flirt with Danny—even have a fling with him—but there would be no long-term commitment. If Danny prized freedom above all else, she would give it to him.

"So," Danny said, standing up and stretching his arms above his head, "what did you want to show me?"

Alissa led him into her room and pointed to the wall opposite the door.

"What do you think of that mirror?"

"The first word that springs to mind is *gaudy*,"

Danny said. "Unless you were going to tell me it's a priceless antique and you love it."

"No." Alissa laughed. "I was hoping you could take it out. It's bolted to the wall somehow."

Danny pulled a small flashlight out of his tool belt and peered behind the mirror. He tugged at the frame from a few different angles, then nodded.

"It should come off with a crowbar, if you don't mind me pulling some of the plaster off."

"That's fine," Alissa said, "I can patch it later."

"I'll get my tools," Danny said.

When he returned a few minutes later, Alissa was arranging painting supplies on a drop cloth, ready to try out samples of the colors she was considering for the walls. It felt natural to be working alongside him again.

"What you were saying before, about walking away…" she began.

"Is this the part where you agree I'm crazy?" Danny asked. He slid the crowbar under the edge of the mirror, gently pushing and pulling to loosen the frame.

"No, not at all," Alissa said. "I think you were brave." She knew how it felt to finally reach all your goals, only to realize your dreams had changed along the way. "Did you just get fed up one day? Do the whole take-this-job-and-shove-it routine?"

"Nothing that dramatic," Danny said. "The thing is…" His voice drifted off. He continued his work on the mirror, his back to Alissa. "My dad got cancer. I said I'd be there for him, but I never showed up for any of his chemo treatments. Too busy with work, closing big deals. They told us he probably had a few years, so I always thought I'd go later. But he was gone in a couple of months. At the end, by the time I got to the hospital, it was too late."

He spoke in a monotone, not trusting himself to say more than the basic facts. She understood why he wouldn't face her.

"My mother died of breast cancer," Alissa said quietly. "Almost two years ago. I was there for all of it. Trust me, you don't want to see someone you love suffer like that."

Danny shook his head. "Not being there is worse. At least, that's how I felt at the funeral. The guilt crushed me—that's the only way I can describe it. I moped around my parents' house, and I called in sick to work for the first time in three years. I felt like I had died, too."

The mirror creaked as he separated a corner of it from the wall. "I dragged myself back to New York eventually," Danny continued, reaching up to slip the crowbar under the frame's top edge. "I didn't care about the mergers or my year-end bonus. I broke up with my girlfriend, quit my job and sold my condo. The only thing I could think to do was come home. My mom was happy to have the company and get help around the house, at least.

"At some point—this was probably about a year ago—I went to the garage and found all my dad's old woodworking tools. I started fooling around again, making tables and shelves. You know that rush you get when you're doing something you really love? It all came back. I realized I really liked working with my hands. I started doing odd jobs for my mom's friends, built some word of mouth, and now here I am."

The top of the mirror popped away from the wall, scattering fragments of plaster on the floor. Danny still hadn't looked at Alissa.

"Thanks for telling me about your dad," she said. "I'm so sorry."

"It's hard to talk about him," Danny said. "But I don't miss anything about my old life. Well—maybe the money."

"I'm sorry, but I don't think I can match an investment bank salary," Alissa said with a laugh.

Danny stood facing the center of the mirror, and Alissa saw his reflection smiling back at her.

"Seriously, I couldn't care less," he said. "I'm so much happier now, it doesn't even compare. That salary kept me chained to a life I hated." He pulled the crowbar with both hands, his shoulder muscles straining with the effort. Then, suddenly, with a loud crack, the mirror fell from the wall, landing with a thump as Danny threw his arms around the sides to soften the impact. While he laid it carefully down on the floor, Alissa went over to take a look.

"Wow," she said. "Do you think that's the original wallpaper?"

She stared at a faded pattern of pink and red roses, surrounded by cracked plaster. Danny came up next to her and leaned in closer.

"Look." He pointed to a narrow seam in the wallpaper. He slid his fingers into the seam and pulled. With a creak, the wall moved.

"A door?" Alissa asked. She peeked through the opening and saw wooden stairs leading up. "Why was this hidden?"

Danny shrugged.

"Where do you think the stairs go?" Alissa asked.

"Only one place they could go," Danny said. "The roof."

CHAPTER SIXTEEN

WILL LEFT EVELYN'S bed at dawn, insisting he had to go before the servants were expected home. Evelyn clung to him nonetheless.

"It won't be long," he said. "By this afternoon, you'll be free of Charles forever."

She walked downstairs with him, watching as he pulled on his still-damp clothes from last night.

"Take these." Will handed her the trousers and shirt she'd taken from Charles's room. "We have to be sure I'm not leaving anything behind."

Evelyn smiled. *Impossible,* she wanted to tell him. *I still feel your kisses on my skin. Wherever I go from now on, I will carry you with me.*

Later that morning, after she'd finished breakfast in her room, Evelyn decided to pack her things so she'd be ready to leave as soon as Will arrived. She dragged a traveling case out from under her bed, one Lavinia had given her as a wedding present. She opened her armoire and stared at the clothes inside. The silk gowns and embroidered shawls Charles had insisted she buy in New York hung undisturbed, like museum exhibits. These luxurious clothes paid for with Brewster money would have no place in her new life. She packed only the simplest cotton dresses and blouses, a few books and her toiletries, including a silver brush and mirror set that had belonged to her grandmother. Everything else could be left behind.

As she folded the clothes on her bed, she was surprised by Mrs. Trimble.

"I've come for your breakfast tray," she said. She stared at the clothes laid out on the bed, the bag on the floor.

"Is Peggy all right?" Evelyn asked. She couldn't remember the housekeeper ever clearing her dishes before.

"I've set her to polishing the silver," Mrs. Trimble said. "She's let the tea service go far too long."

"Over there." Evelyn pointed to her bedside table. Mrs. Trimble waited a moment too long before moving toward the tray. Evelyn knew the woman was curious, but she fought the urge to offer an excuse. It had taken her months to learn that the lady of the house owed her staff no explanations.

Everything Evelyn deemed necessary fit in the one bag. After it was buckled shut, she was left with hours to fill. She ate lunch alone in the dining room, picking nervously at the sliced chicken and potato salad. She took one last stroll around the garden, reliving her moments here with Will. Back inside, she was trying to distract herself with a book when there was a knock on the front door.

She rushed to open it, and it was all she could do not to throw herself into Will's arms. He smiled at her with delight. "It's all arranged," he whispered. "My car's outside."

"Let me get my things," Evelyn said. Her hands trembled as she closed the door behind him.

Evelyn raced to her bedroom and picked up her bag. She took a quick glance around the room. So many memories here, only one of them happy. But that night with Will was enough to overshadow all the others. As she took her bag downstairs, she saw Peggy crossing the foyer holding a tray with two china cups.

"What are you doing, Peggy?" she asked.

"Mrs. Trimble saw Mr. Brewster was here—Mr. William, that is—and she said I should offer refreshments. If you think he'd prefer coffee, I could serve that as well, though it will take longer…."

"I don't think Mr. William plans on staying," Evelyn said.

Peggy nodded and turned back to the kitchen. Now that the moment was here, Evelyn felt time slow to an unendurable crawl. She was so close. To be denied escape now would be unbearable. She entered the parlor and saw Will sitting in an armchair, staring into the fireplace. She remembered lying with him on the floor, only a few feet away. She could still conjure up the feel of her hands as they moved along his back, warmed by the heat of the flames.

She stood next to him. Her fingers trailed lightly over his shoulder.

"I wish I could kiss you," Will said quietly.

"I know." They both looked over at the fireplace, and Evelyn knew he was remembering that night. Already, it seemed, they could communicate without words.

"I'm ready," Evelyn said. "Where are we going?"

"Indianapolis," Will said. "I have a friend from school who married a girl out there, some sort of corn heiress. I don't suppose she'll let us stay with them, given the scandal that will follow, but he can be trusted to find us a discreet place for a day or two. No one will think to look for us there, and it will give us time to decide where to go next. I was thinking perhaps California."

"California?" It might as well have been China. Evelyn knew nothing about California other than stories of the Gold Rush. To her it was a place beyond the frontier, teetering on the very edge of the earth. Still, its isolation was a point in its favor. No one there would know anything about the Brewsters.

The sound of horses and carriage wheels startled them to attention. They both knew, even before their eyes met in horror, that it must be Charles. Immediately, Will stood, as if to protect Evelyn, but she brushed past him. She needed to confront her husband herself.

The front door swung open as Evelyn entered the foyer. There she found Charles, looking for a moment as dashing as the day she first met him. His hair had been brushed back and pomaded so it lay smooth against his head. His suit and coat hung immaculately from his tall frame. Then she saw the contempt in his eyes. Whatever had attracted her to him once had been extinguished long ago.

"Dear wife," he said with exaggerated courtesy. "Ah, Will. I thought that was your car out front."

Will nodded briefly toward his brother. "Charles."

"So, it's a family gathering, is it?" Charles asked. "Strange. I never received an invitation."

"I thought you were in Washington," Evelyn said.

"Indeed I was," Charles said, "until I received some very disturbing news. Something that demanded my immediate attention."

Evelyn allowed herself a flicker of hope. If Charles was distracted by business, she and Will might still have a chance to get away.

"Mrs. Trimble!" Charles called out. Evelyn turned to see the housekeeper enter the foyer. The older woman stared fixedly at Charles.

"I must thank you for your loyalty," Charles told her. "You will be well compensated for it." He flashed Evelyn and Will a wide, dangerous smile. "I was most concerned to hear that my brother was lurking around my garden, so very early in the morning. What could have been the reason?"

Evelyn heard Will's breathing quicken. The Trimbles' cottage, perched at the edge of the property, looked out over the open field Will would have walked through on his way home this morning. He had made that journey so many times before, but always at night, when the darkness concealed his movements and the Trimbles' curtains were closed. But today one of them could easily have seen Will pass by in the distance. They had a telephone. They would have called Alma. And Alma would not have hesitated to tell Charles.

"Mrs. Trimble, you may have the rest of the day off," Charles said, waving his hand in dismissal. "Tell the women in the kitchen as well."

As Mrs. Trimble's heels clicked away across the marble, Will took a step toward his brother. Evelyn shook her head. Not yet.

"Charles," she said, "you know as well as I do that our marriage is a failure. I've asked for a divorce, which you've denied me. I'm left with no other course of action. I'm leaving."

Charles laughed. "Leaving?"

"Yes, today," Evelyn continued. She had to keep talking. If her words tumbled out fast enough, they might stun him into silence. She might win just enough time to walk out the door. "I believe the legal term is abandonment. I'm prepared to stay away as long as I must, until you are willing—"

"Enough!" Charles shouted. "It's time you learned your place!" He reached for her, but Will threw himself between them and grabbed Charles's shoulders, pushing him out of the way.

"Don't touch her," Will growled, gritting his teeth from the effort.

The rest happened so suddenly that later Evelyn could only remember it as a blur of action. With a burst of fury, Charles flung himself at his brother, slamming Will's body sideways. Will, disoriented, tried to stand, but Charles punched him in the jaw, then pulled open the front door as Will struggled to catch his breath. With a strength fueled by rage, Charles shoved his brother out the door, throwing him onto the porch. He turned the lock as Will's fists began to beat against the heavy oak panels.

"Let me in!" Will shouted.

"So much for your noble prince," Charles said, looking at Evelyn with disgust. "Good God, I've been a fool. You parade around as the virtuous wronged wife, when all along you've been sleeping with my own brother! Even I couldn't have imagined such a betrayal."

"It's not what you think," Evelyn protested.

"It's exactly what I think," Charles said, taking a step closer.

"Evelyn!" Will called from outside. "Evelyn!"

"I think perhaps I'll punish you here," Charles said. "Do you think your lover would enjoy overhearing what I do to you?"

Evelyn looked around in a panic. She had so little time. She could run for the kitchen and throw herself behind Mrs. Gower. But the servants had probably slipped out the back door by now. Even if the cook or Peggy had stayed behind, they would offer no protection. Charles was capable of killing them all in his frenzy to get to her.

"Evelyn!" Will shouted again. "Get away from him! I'll help you, I promise, just run!"

Charles turned around and slammed his palm against the front door. "Get out of here!" he screamed. "You'll never touch her again!"

In that instant, Evelyn saw her chance. Charles would catch her if she tried to run through the parlor, but she might reach the stairs before him. She had only a second to act. As Charles faced the door, shouting at Will, she flung herself at the stairs, grabbing at the banister. She jumped to the third step, then raced the rest of the way. Charles's footsteps stomped close behind her. She propelled herself into the bedroom and slammed the door closed behind her. Her fingers trembled as they slid the lock sideways.

"You won't lock me out again!" Charles shouted. "You idiot! You think I can't break this door down?"

Evelyn raced to the other side of the bedroom. She

pulled open the French doors and ran onto the balcony. Could she jump? She stared at the flagstones on the patio below. It would be a long, hard fall.

"Mrs. Gower!" she shouted into the void. "Peggy!" There was no answer from the kitchen windows beneath her.

"You won't keep me out!" Charles shouted. Evelyn heard the sound of his continued assault on the door. The wood panels shuddered with the force of his blows.

She was trapped. She could lock herself in the bathroom, but it wouldn't take long for him to break that door as well. She could jump from the balcony, a fall that might do as much damage as Charles's fists. There was one other choice, but the escape it offered would be fleeting. If she took the hidden staircase up to the roof, she would be at Charles's mercy at the very top of the house.

Over the cracking wood, Evelyn heard the faint sound of Will's voice, calling her name.

At that moment, the bedroom door broke off its hinges. Charles stumbled into the doorway, staggering as he tried to right himself. Will was on his way. But not fast enough. Evelyn had to give him enough time to reach her.

She pulled open the narrow door in the wall and flung it closed behind her. There was no lock; Charles would be behind her in seconds. If she could get a head start on the rooftop walkway, it might be enough. By now, Will would be racing up the front stairs to get to her. By the time she reached the roof, he might already be in her bedroom....

It was a gloomy, overcast afternoon, and Evelyn clutched the railing with both hands as she hurried along the narrow wood planks. She'd always loved the view of Oak Hill from here, a collection of tiny dollhouses. It seemed impossible that this nightmare could be unfolding in such a peaceful setting. Evelyn had gone halfway around the roof before she realized she was still alone. Charles had been right behind her in the bedroom. He must have seen her come up here. Where was he? And where was Will? Shivering with fear and cold, she waited.

When the footsteps came, they were slow and deliberate. It had to be Will—he must have stopped Charles, somehow, and was now coming to rescue her. Still, she remained motionless. When she peered around the edge of the rooftop and saw Charles's dark hair emerging from the door to the stairs, she almost cried out. As he walked toward her, a flash of silver caught her eye. He was carrying something in his hand.

"Evelyn!" Charles exclaimed, as if surprised to find her in such an unexpected spot. "Surely you see there is nowhere left to hide."

She remained silent, waiting. As he approached, she recognized the silver object as a gun.

He smiled, acknowledging her fear. "Ah, yes, this old relic. Haven't you seen it before? But then, you never spent much time in my office, did you? It's my grandfather's dueling pistol—as if the old man ever had to fight for his honor. Despite its age, it still fires remarkably well. Yes, I've tried it. Not in a duel, of course, although perhaps that might be one way out of this mess. Shall I challenge Will to a duel? Would that satisfy you?"

"Charles," Evelyn said, trying to keep her tone level. "There's no need for a gun."

"There wouldn't be, if you hadn't felt the need to be so dramatic. Running away from me like a lunatic! You forget that you brought all this on yourself by inviting my brother into your bed."

"I'm so sorry." She would say anything to make him lower the gun.

"So, will you stop this ridiculousness, and follow me back to the house? We should be able to talk this over as adults."

"Yes." Evelyn knew he didn't want to talk. But if she gave in to him now, he might let her live.

It was so quiet in that moment, as Charles slowly lowered the gun and waited for her to approach. Then the stillness was broken by Will's thundering footsteps. Evelyn opened her mouth to warn him about the gun, but before she could say a word, Charles whirled around and pulled the trigger. The crack of gunfire exploded through the sky, and Will fell. Evelyn couldn't even scream.

But then, seconds later, she saw that Will wasn't dead. Not even hurt, because he was standing again, running and tackling Charles, knocking the gun from his brother's hands. The gun clattered against the rooftop before falling down to the front drive. The men twisted together in a fight so intense that Evelyn couldn't distinguish who was who. She could only hear the grunting of their breath. She stood, frozen, as they kicked and punched and groaned.

And then, suddenly, one pushed against the other with such force that a wood beam supporting the railing cracked. The punches continued, and the support post snapped from the impact of the body slammed against it. The railing came apart, and Evelyn watched as

Charles rolled off the walkway into the emptiness beyond. A single scream rang out before ending in a sickening thud.

Will pulled himself up onto all fours and crawled toward Evelyn. She couldn't stop shaking as he folded her into his arms.

"What happened?" she mumbled against his chest, the words tangling in her tongue. "Where is he?"

"He's gone."

It was over. Charles wouldn't come for her ever again.

"Did he hurt you?" Will asked, moving his hands along her shoulders and arms, checking she was still intact.

"I had to run around to the back door," Will murmured. "I came as fast as I could, my darling. I was so afraid I'd be too late."

They huddled together in silence, but Evelyn's mind was racing. Her husband's body was lying in the front drive. A gun would be found somewhere nearby. The wood railings were broken where Charles had fallen through. The servants knew Will had been in the house earlier. Someone would have heard the gunshot. All these pieces of information jumbled together, then arranged themselves in a disturbing pattern. She grabbed Will's hands.

"Will, you need to go," she pleaded.

"Why?" he asked. "I'm not leaving you. Come, we'll go to the station right now, as we planned."

"Don't you see how that will look? If we disappear now, leaving Charles behind like this? They'll come after us and we'll never be free."

Will sighed. "You're right. I suppose we should call

the police. And Mother. Oh, my God, what will I tell her?" Will's shoulders slumped, and Evelyn saw the exhaustion of his fight with Charles etched into his face.

Evelyn fought to keep her thoughts focused. She could work it out, but there was so little time.

"No, you can't stay," Evelyn said. "Everything points to you, don't you see? You were fighting with Charles, and he was pushed off the roof. You and I can insist it was an accident, but you could be charged with murder anyway."

Will stared at her. "But it *was* an accident. You know that, don't you?"

"Of course," Evelyn said. "You saved my life. But think how it will seem to someone who wasn't here. Who's to say you weren't the one holding the gun? Charles is the pride of the family. Even your mother may speak against you."

"She'll need someone to blame. The thought of facing her—"

"You won't have to." Evelyn cut him off. "I'll say it was my fault. A tragic accident during a domestic argument."

"But I can't leave you here, to bear all that alone."

"You need to. It's the only way. You must leave town as soon as possible." Evelyn thought for a moment, then continued. "I'll say you stopped at the house to say goodbye to me before leaving on a journey west. You cut your visit short when Charles came home in a foul temper. You left for the train station, and that was the last I saw of you. If I tell a story close enough to the truth, I may even be treated with sympathy."

"Not by Mother," Will said. "Evelyn—don't underestimate her anger."

Evelyn nodded. "I don't know what she'll do. Still, the family's reputation is sacred. She may hate me in private, but she'll do anything to avoid a public scandal."

Will considered her plan, then nodded. "If you're sure."

"I am. It's the only way."

"I'll send word as soon as I'm able," Will promised. "We'll start afresh, just as we planned."

They stood and walked carefully back to the door, then down the stairs to Evelyn's bedroom, clinging to each other all the while. The house was quiet.

"Peggy! Mrs. Gower!" Evelyn called. There was no answer. Although she'd been hurt by their desertion earlier, she saw now it was for the best. No one would know that Will had been here when Charles died.

"Go, go," Evelyn urged, as they approached the front door.

"There's one thing I have to do first," Will said. He opened the door and went outside. Evelyn watched him peer from side to side on the porch, then hurry off to the right. In a moment he was back, his expression grim.

"I had to be sure about Charles," Will said. "He's dead."

Evelyn stepped back inside. She didn't want to see what was lying in her front garden.

Will gathered her in his arms. "Never forget that I love you," he whispered against her neck. "Promise you'll come to me."

"I will. As soon as I can." They kissed, slowly and sadly, a kiss drained of the fire of their previous embraces.

Evelyn watched Will climb into his car and drive off. She felt more alone than ever before. In a few moments, she would take responsibility for her husband's death. If her plan failed and she had to tell the truth instead, there was no way of reaching Will to ask for his help. There would be no witness to confirm her side of the story. Will could disappear forever, leaving her to pay the price.

Evelyn thought of Charles's body only a few feet away. She closed the front door and ran to the telephone in the parlor.

"Operator!"

"Mrs. Brewster? How are you this evening?"

Evelyn recognized the voice. It was Agnes, a chatty woman who treated the Brewster family like royalty.

"Please, call the police," Evelyn said. Her voice shook. She wouldn't have to put on an act to sound upset. Already, tears were welling up in her eyes. "There's been a terrible accident."

CHAPTER SEVENTEEN

ALISSA STOOD with Danny on the wooden walkway at the top of the house. She looked out over the surrounding landscape: the town of Oak Hill directly in front of them, trees and fields intersected by country roads in the distance. Off to the left, the highway cut a dark gash through the grass. Alissa clutched the railing with both hands, unnerved by the height.

"I can't think of any other house around here with an overlook like this," Danny said.

"If we were closer to the water, I'd call it a widow's walk," Alissa commented. "You know—the place where women would watch for their husbands who'd gone to sea."

Danny stared out at the horizon. "All that used to be Brewster property," he said. "Maybe they wanted a place to gloat." He walked farther out, then stopped, leaning over to examine the railing more closely.

"What is it?" Alissa asked.

"Look here." Danny pointed to the section in front of him. "Most of the wood up here is cedar. Pretty expensive, especially for a part of the house most people would never see. But this part is cheap pine. Shoddy workmanship, too. You can see the nails sticking out."

Alissa decided it wasn't worth walking out to see for herself. Straying too far from the doorway made her nervous. She told Danny she'd see him back downstairs, and he followed her to the bedroom shortly afterward.

"Looks like it was a rush repair job," he said. "The original railing must've broken somehow."

Suddenly, Alissa pictured a body crashing through those narrow beams as the wood disintegrated. It would be a three-story fall to the ground below. In the dark, Charles could have lost his footing easily. Would he have realized what was happening or would it have been too fast? Evelyn could have been here in the bedroom when her husband climbed those stairs for the last time. Had she heard him scream?

Or maybe it was more sinister. If Roger Blake was right, Evelyn might have followed Charles to the roof. The railing was so thin, it wouldn't have taken much to push a man through if he was caught off guard. Alissa didn't want to believe it, but it was possible.

Evelyn. It always came back to Evelyn. Where had she gone? Why had she left the house?

Of course. The house. A person could vanish, but real estate didn't. Turning to Danny, Alissa asked breathlessly, "How late do you think government offices stay open?"

"I don't know," he replied, puzzled. "Five o'clock?"

Alissa glanced at her watch. "I think we can make it. Meet you downstairs—I've got to look up an address on my laptop."

"What about this?" Danny asked, pointing to the staircase behind him.

Alissa doubted she'd ever go to the roof again. She certainly didn't want that doorway in her bedroom as a daily reminder of what she suspected had happened up there.

"We'll plaster over it," she said. "But it can wait. C'mon."

Danny looked down at his sweaty T-shirt and filthy jeans. He saw Alissa's bright eyes watching him expectantly, and his exhaustion lifted. He suspected this mystery trip would end in yet another dead end, and he dreaded seeing Alissa disappointed again. But she was reaching out to him, and for now, that was enough. Maybe that kiss in the kitchen had meant something to her after all.

"Where exactly are we going?" he asked as he followed Alissa from the bedroom.

"We have to find out what happened to the house after Charles died," Alissa called to him as she raced down the stairs. At the bottom, she turned and stared up at him.

"Don't you see?" she asked urgently, as if the force of her words could propel him faster. "There has to be a paper trail. It might tell us where Evelyn went."

THE HOME-OWNERSHIP records for the town of Oak Hill were kept in the basement of the county courthouse. A cheerful young woman who looked like she belonged in high school appeared delighted to welcome visitors to her dimly lit domain. The ID tag clipped to the waist of her skirt identified her as Polly Martinez.

"What can I help you with?" she asked Alissa and Danny in a jarringly peppy voice.

Alissa gave Polly her address and said she was looking for the home's records. Once the clerk realized the records in question went back a hundred years, her face fell.

"Oh, we've got some digging to do," she said. "Those will be in the storeroom somewhere."

The storeroom turned out to be a long, narrow space lit by only a few hanging bulbs. Industrial metal shelves formed three narrow aisles, and were stacked with identical brown storage boxes. The clerk led Alissa and Danny down one aisle before climbing on a step stool to peer at the labels on the boxes above their heads.

"Okay, here are the records for Oak Hill," Polly said finally. She dragged a box from the shelf. Danny reached up to take it from her, then placed it on a table at the edge of the room. The young woman opened the box and rummaged around inside, eventually pulling out a large book bound in green leather.

"This covers the years from 1900 to 1965," she said. "From 1965 to 1985, the records are in this other ledger." She pointed to another, similar book. "After that, we've got everything on the computer."

"Great," Alissa said, taking a seat at the table. "We'll start with these."

Polly opened the first book. "The addresses are organized geographically, so you'll have to find your street first."

"I'm sure we can figure it out." Alissa smiled politely but she was impatient to get started. She leaned over the book and began flipping through the pages as Danny watched over her shoulder. Handwritten addresses were listed in the first column on each page, followed by dates of sale and the names of both buyers and sellers.

A fair number of addresses on each page had no sale date listed. Many families in Oak Hill, it seemed, lived in the same house all their lives.

"What does this mean?" Danny asked, pointing to a notation that reappeared occasionally.

"The letter *T* means the deed was transferred to another name without a sale," Polly said. "Usually when a house was left to someone in a will. We close in half an hour, so I'll let you get to work. I've got to get back and cover the phone."

Alissa hadn't heard the phone ring since they arrived, but she nodded and said they'd be fine. She turned through the pages, pausing when she saw familiar street names. Her eyes scanned the entries until she saw her street, Washington Drive. But her address, number fifty, wasn't listed.

"Where's the house?" she asked, mystified.

Danny looked over the page, trying to reconcile hundred-year-old addresses with the town he knew.

"None of the houses around yours are in here, either," he said. "It looks like Washington ran for only a few blocks."

"Oh, I know!" Alissa declared. "The house wasn't part of the town back then. It was on the Brewster estate. How do we find that?"

Frustrated, she flipped to the end of the Oak Hill listings. The next section was headed Oak Hill Environs. And there she saw it, written in precise, angular handwriting: Edward Brewster and Alma Brewster home, Brewster Drive. The first date that appeared after the address was 1910, when the property was transferred to Lavinia and Winslow Preston.

Charles's sister and her husband. They must have moved into the mansion after Charles's mother died. The next date marked a sale, in 1945, to the Sisters of St. Mary Mercy. The home was sold to the State of Maryland in 1962, followed by one last entry: Demolished, 1963.

Alissa moved to the next line: Winslow and Lavinia Preston home, Brewster Drive. The home was sold in 1910 to a Mr. J. Clayton Marsh. It had been sold a few times afterward until, like the main house, it was demolished in 1963.

On the next line, she saw it: Charles Brewster home, Brewster Drive. Alissa pointed to the words, and Danny nodded.

"Why isn't Evelyn listed as an owner?" Alissa asked. "The other wives were."

"Maybe Charles moved in before he got married," Danny suggested.

Her heart racing, Alissa stared at the page, searching for a clue to what had happened next. But there was no mention of a change in owners in 1905, the year Charles died. Only a few blank lines, followed by a notation that the house passed to Lavinia in 1910, then Beatrice Healey in 1950. The name sounded vaguely familiar. Alissa tried to remember the newspaper clippings she'd copied at the library. Beatrice. Lavinia's daughter. A few years later, ownership was transferred to the Paulson Trust at the First National Bank of San Francisco.

"What do you think this is?" Alissa asked. "A charity?"

"I guess," Danny said. "But why would a group in California want a house in Maryland?"

"Let's keep going." Alissa closed the book and

picked up the next ledger, covering the years 1965 to 1985. After some fruitless flipping back and forth, Alissa realized that her house might be listed under its current street address, since the Brewster estate no longer existed. Sure enough, she found an entry for 50 Washington Street. In 1973, the San Francisco bank sold the property to Samuel and Melody Foster.

"Do you know them?" Danny asked.

Alissa nodded. "I haven't met her, but Melody Foster's name was on the papers when I bought the house. She lived there with her sister."

This was it, the end of the trail. Alissa closed the ledger, keeping her head bent so Danny wouldn't see her disappointment. Respecting her silence, Danny carefully placed the books back in the storage box. He put a hand on her shoulder and gave a quick squeeze.

"They're about to shut off the lights on us," he said. "Wanna grab some dinner?"

Alissa shook her head. "Thanks, but I just want to go home."

She stood abruptly, anxious to escape the dim, claustrophobic room. She tossed a quick thank-you to Polly at the front desk before hurrying down the front steps of the courthouse with Danny trailing behind.

It wasn't until they were on the highway that Alissa felt up to talking.

"I can't believe I was so stupid," she lamented. "Thinking I'd find some overlooked will or letter in a dusty old basement."

"It was worth a try," Danny said.

"According to those records, Evelyn never existed. The harder I try to find her, the further away she gets."

Danny tried to change the subject by talking about his search for a decent electrician, but Alissa answered in monosyllables. Given her morose mood, she assumed Danny would make a hasty getaway when they returned to the house. Instead, he waited by the car as Alissa walked around from the driver's side.

"I've got a surprise for you," he said. Even if it was only a ploy to distract her, Alissa managed a smile to show she appreciated the effort.

She followed Danny through the foyer and along the hallway past the dining room. Pushing open the door to the kitchen, he ushered her in with a dramatic flourish. Alissa stopped, stunned by the bright, open space in front of her.

"I installed the last of the cabinets this morning," Danny said, leaning against the doorway and grinning proudly.

For the first time in months, the room looked like a kitchen rather than a workshop. Late-afternoon sunlight poured through French doors that had been installed in the opposite wall, looking out over the garden. Danny had removed the plastic sheeting that had hidden the floor, revealing the new hardwood below. Smiling with delight, Alissa opened cupboards and drawers and declared everything perfect. The walls still needed a coat of paint and the ancient yellow stove had yet to be replaced, but the kitchen had become what she'd envisioned: a place that welcomed her.

"This calls for a celebration." Alissa took a half-empty bottle of white wine from the fridge, and Danny found some plastic cups by the sink. After they toasted the new kitchen, Alissa suggested going outside. Pulling open the French doors, they walked out to the patio and settled in two Adirondack chairs Alissa had found at a secondhand store and refinished.

"Thanks for coming with me today," Alissa said. "Even if it was a total waste of time."

"I'm sure you'll come up with some other way to track down the mysterious Evelyn Brewster." Danny covered her hand reassuringly with his own.

"I don't think so," Alissa said. "It's not like I can hire a private investigator to find someone who vanished a hundred years ago."

Danny laughed.

"What?" Alissa asked defensively.

"Listen to you," he said. "Does it really matter?"

Alissa felt her face flush. Gearing up to defend herself, she saw the gentleness in Danny's eyes, the way he leaned back calmly in his chair. He wasn't mocking her. He was simply asking a question. Did it matter?

"Maybe that wacko Roger is right and the woman killed her husband," Danny said. "Or maybe not. Either way, he died, and it's a sad story, but it's over."

"I can't explain it," Alissa said, "but I feel like they're still here, somehow."

"Now that's more like it." Danny's eyes sparkled with amusement. "You've seen the ghost of Charles Brewster!"

Alissa laughed along, but the truth was more complicated. She'd sensed a certain spirit in the house from the very beginning, but it was never threatening. The house had always made her feel safe. As if she belonged here.

"Forget about the Brewsters," Danny said.

He leaned over toward her, his voice urgent. "You've earned this place, don't you see? I've never seen an owner work as hard as you have. It's not the Brewster house anymore. It's yours."

Alissa let the words sink in as she watched the fading sunlight shimmer through the trees. She might never find out exactly how Charles Brewster died. She might never know what happened to Evelyn Brewster. She would have to be at peace with that.

Danny was still leaning toward her, holding his empty cup in one hand. Alissa couldn't know for sure what would happen between her and Danny. But she realized with a rush that the house felt most like home when he was there with her. The Brewsters belonged to the past. Her new life was just beginning.

Alissa took the cup from Danny's hand and met him halfway. Reaching across the space between them, they kissed so intensely that Alissa forgot about Evelyn and Charles, forgot about the list of repair projects that hovered constantly in the back of her mind. Tonight, she wanted to be with Danny. Everything else could wait.

This time, Danny was the one who pulled away. He looked at Alissa, his concern written on his face.

"Do you know what you're doing?" he asked.

Alissa shook her head. "No."

"Good. Me neither."

They laughed, and in her mind, Alissa could already hear the words they would say later that night: "I love you." For the first time in months, she felt free. She was in a place she loved with a man she loved. The rest would work itself out.

CHAPTER EIGHTEEN

IN THE DAYS immediately after Charles's death, Evelyn kept herself isolated from the rest of the family. The events of that dreadful afternoon unfolded again and again in her mind. The policemen arriving, examining Charles's body. One of them coming back to the house, holding the gun, asking her if she recognized it. The silent walk to the mansion to break the news to her mother-in-law. Alma's face, shifting from confusion to horror. Her features tightening with rage as she cried out, eyes fixed on Evelyn: "What did you do?"

Evelyn turned away, terrified Alma might mistake her fear for guilt. She ran home, sobbing so heavily that pain rippled through her chest. When two policemen knocked on her front door the next morning, Evelyn assumed they had been sent on Alma's orders to question her further. She recognized the younger one, who had inspected the body the day before. The older man introduced himself as Detective Collier and apologized for intruding and treated her with gentle sympathy.

He asked Evelyn to repeat her account of what had happened and wrote down her statement in a small notebook.

"This is very helpful," he said reassuringly. "I'm sorry to trouble you. However, it is important that we make our inquiries as close as possible to the time of the incident."

Evelyn wondered if Alma had voiced any suspicions about her. "My mother-in-law," she said carefully. "She was quite distraught when I told her."

The detective nodded. "I've spoken with Mrs. Brewster. She feels the loss deeply, as any mother would." He leaned in closer, lowering his voice. "I've made inquiries in town, and more than one person has mentioned Mr. Brewster's temper. A person of that disposition doesn't always think clearly. He may act rashly, with no thought to the consequences. Would you agree?"

Evelyn nodded mutely, afraid to guess at his meaning.

"Based on our conversation, I'm prepared to file a report of accidental death. For Mrs. Brewster's sake— and your own—there won't be any mention of the gun, or possible difficulties between you and Mr. Brewster. However, I must tell you, in strictest confidence, I think you're quite a brave woman. It can't have been easy, living with such a man."

Evelyn looked down at the floor. "Thank you."

She was safe. No matter what Alma might suspect, she would never risk a public scandal. Still, Evelyn kept her distance. She received stacks of condolence cards, many from people she'd never met, but there were few visitors. As if death were contagious, friends and neighbors stayed away. Evelyn curtly told Mrs. Trimble that her services were no longer required.

"As you wish, ma'am." The housekeeper's face

remained impassive as ever, oblivious to the tragedy her actions had caused.

Mrs. Gower and Peggy remained, tending to Evelyn and offering occasional meals, which Evelyn barely ate. Her mother tried to convince her to move back to town.

"You shouldn't be here alone," Katherine said.

"I can't leave," Evelyn insisted. "Not until I hear from Will."

The only other person who came to the house was Lavinia, who informed Evelyn of the funeral plans and offered to lend her a black dress. When Lavinia announced that it would be best if she arrived at the funeral on her own rather than riding in the family carriage— an order that could only have come from Alma—she had the decency to look embarrassed. Evelyn agreed, then asked if she could see Beatrice. Lavinia shook her head decisively.

"That wouldn't be appropriate."

Alma had arranged for the funeral to be held at one of Baltimore's largest churches, correctly predicting that hundreds would turn out to bid farewell to Charles Brewster. When Evelyn arrived, she was escorted to the front pew, where the rest of the family had already been seated. Alma stared at the altar straight in front of her, refusing to acknowledge Evelyn's presence. Evelyn walked past her mother-in-law and Lavinia and sat down next to Winslow, who gave her a sympathetic nod.

"A sad day," he said. "We're all that's left of the clan now, I suppose."

The grand Brewster family didn't even fill half a pew.

"Shame about Will," Winslow said.

"What?" Evelyn's voice rose with concern. "What happened to him?"

Winslow looked confused. "I only meant, it's terrible to think he knows nothing of his brother's death. You don't happen to know where he took off to, do you?"

"I wish I did," Evelyn said quietly. Winslow looked at her curiously.

"You were always great friends, weren't you?" he asked.

Evelyn looked down at her hands, encased in black gloves. She knew something in her tone had already revealed too much.

"Ah, well, it's a shame Will felt the need to be so mysterious," Winslow continued. "Lavinia has exhausted herself trying to find him."

Lavinia did appear to be on the verge of collapse. Evelyn had never felt close to her sister-in-law, but she felt a stab of sympathy. One of Lavinia's brothers was dead. The other was missing. Grief had turned her active, capable mother to stone. If things had been different between them, Evelyn would have taken Lavinia's hand. As it was, the gulf between them was too vast.

The service passed in a haze of speeches and hymns. Evelyn shook hands with people at the back of the church afterward, then took her carriage home. She knew missing the reception at Alma's was a scandalous breach of etiquette, but what more could the Brewsters do to her? She was already a pariah.

The days dragged by, with no word from Will. Evelyn paced through the house, unwilling to leave in case a telegram or letter arrived. The world went on without her. Somewhere, Will was starting a new life while she lived like a prisoner. She hadn't slept a full night since Charles's death.

One week after the funeral, Evelyn received a curt note from Alma, requesting her presence at a family conference to discuss Charles's will. Evelyn approached the main house the next day with a combination of dread and anticipation. She didn't expect Charles to leave her a fortune—he'd never been a generous man—but there would be some sort of settlement.

Evelyn greeted the butler, Hayes, at the front door and walked down the long, high-ceilinged hallway. She passed the doorway to the dining room, where she'd gathered for so many family dinners. How many times had she passed through this hall with Charles, her heart racing at the thought of seeing Will again? Alma's sitting room was at the end of the hall. Evelyn walked in and saw her mother-in-law, Lavinia and Winslow sitting in silence.

"Ah, hello, Evelyn," Winslow said in a weak imitation of his usual hearty greeting. Lavinia nodded silently. Alma turned away with a grimace, as if the sight of her daughter-in-law caused physical pain. Evelyn pulled up a wooden side chair and sat down opposite Alma.

"Now that we're all here, there are business matters to attend to," Alma said. Her tone was as imperious as ever, but she looked as if duty alone was keeping her going. Her face, always sharp and thin, was now haggard, and her skin looked gray. Her once-haughty shoulders stooped forward. The brittle outer shell of Alma Brewster was crumbling away, revealing the old woman inside.

"Winslow," she began, "I am grateful to you for taking the reins at the office. Brewster Shipping must live on, as a legacy to my husband and son."

"Rest assured, it will," Winslow said. "I sent the letter we discussed, introducing myself to the most important customers. Next week, I'll go to New York and Philadelphia to smooth things over."

"Thank you," Alma said. "It is a great relief to know the business is in good hands. Lavinia—are you still sorting through the correspondence?"

"Yes, Mother. I've put aside those letters you should answer personally."

"Any of interest?"

Lavinia nodded. "A letter from the governor arrived yesterday. Written in his own hand."

"How gratifying." Alma stared straight ahead, lost in thought, as if she were gathering strength for the rest of the conversation. Then she turned to Evelyn.

"No doubt you're curious about the will," she said coldly.

Taken aback, Evelyn protested, "I never—"

Alma waved a hand to silence her. "Due to your family background, our lawyers had some concerns about Charles's will after his marriage." More than likely, Evelyn guessed, it had been Alma who was concerned, not the lawyers. "The deed to your house remains in my name. Charles's money and property were to be left to his heirs. In the unlikely event the marriage was childless—" she looked at Evelyn meaningfully, holding her responsible for this unfortunate result "—Charles's fortune was to be left in trust to his nearest relative, his sister, Lavinia."

Evelyn refused to look away. The silence continued, becoming steadily more unbearable.

Then, perhaps because she was disappointed by Evelyn's lack of reaction, Alma spat out her next words. "You won't get a penny."

Evelyn stood. Her immediate impulse was to run out of the room. Anything to escape Alma's hatred. But running away would only confirm every suspicion the Brewsters had about her. Somehow, she must leave with dignity.

"I have no interest in Charles's money," Evelyn said. "I never did."

"I have every right to insist you leave the house immediately," Alma said.

"Mother—" Lavinia began, looking frantically between Alma and Evelyn. "You wouldn't put a widow out on the street."

"Thank you, Lavinia, but I would prefer to leave," Evelyn said. "If I could ask for a day to put my things in order?"

Alma nodded. "As of today, I will no longer be paying the servants' wages," she said. "Your accounts at the grocer's and other shops have been closed."

"I would expect no less." Evelyn struggled to keep her tone neutral. She addressed Lavinia. "Might I say goodbye to Beatrice before I leave? You know I care for her a great deal."

Before Lavinia had a chance to respond, Alma broke in. "You will stay away from my granddaughter. You've brought enough pain to this family." Alma didn't even look at Evelyn as she said the devastating words.

"I'll be gone tomorrow," Evelyn said to Lavinia, then

walked out of the room. As she left the house, Evelyn's hurt and anger faded. Instead, she felt pity. Alma had lost her favorite child, the one on whom she'd pinned all her hopes. Evelyn could start her life over, but Alma would never recover.

Despite the biting wind, Evelyn decided to walk home over the open fields. She traced the route Will had followed so many times, pushing through the same tall grass to reach her garden. She watched her house grow steadily larger over the horizon, the house that was no longer hers. She arrived at the edge of the property, her feet moving more quickly across the clipped lawn. She approached the garden room and stepped inside. With the tree bare of leaves, it felt stark and empty.

For a moment, she missed Will so intensely it hurt. She felt under the stone bench. Nothing, of course. It was ridiculous to think Will might have somehow left a note. He was across the country by now. But she'd sensed his presence here, in the place that had been theirs.

Evelyn turned away from the bench and returned to the house. As she came through the parlor, Peggy rushed toward her.

"Is it true? Are we being turned out?" she asked in a panicky voice.

"I'm afraid so," Evelyn said. "I'm sorry it's come to this."

"I'm told I'll have my wages paid tomorrow, then I'm on my own."

"I'm sure I could put in a good word with Lavinia," Evelyn offered. "Perhaps she could use another girl on her staff."

Peggy shook her head. "Begging your pardon, but I have no interest in working for Mrs. Preston. Or at the main house. I thought I might find a position in Baltimore. Do you think I could do that? Would a city family hire someone like me?"

"Of course they would. I'll write you a letter of reference."

Peggy sniffed and blinked quickly, stifling tears. "It's been a pleasure working for you, Mrs. Brewster. Where will you go?"

"I'll stay with my mother for now," Evelyn told her. "Then, who knows?"

"Will you need help with your things?"

Evelyn shook her head. The bag she'd packed to run off with Will was still sitting in her bedroom. She could be gone in a matter of minutes. But she wanted one last night to make peace with what had happened here.

"Mrs. Gower says to tell you she'll prepare dinner tonight, then say her goodbyes," Peggy said. "Oh—I almost forgot. This telegram came for you."

She handed Evelyn a Western Union envelope. Evelyn ripped into the paper and read the message eagerly.

Meet me in San Francisco. Bay Hotel. Miss you desperately. Come soon. Will.

San Francisco! Evelyn's heart began to race. He made it sound so simple. She would have to travel across the country for days by herself to reach him. They had very little money, and faced an uncertain future. But none of it mattered. He missed her desperately. Evelyn had tried so hard to be strong. Now, she wondered how much longer she could hold on without him.

"Good news?" Peggy asked.

"Yes, very," Evelyn said.

"Time you were happy." Understanding flashed briefly between them. Peggy might be flighty, but she was a good enough servant to keep her mistress's secrets.

THE NEXT MORNING, Evelyn walked through the empty house. So many terrible things had happened here, but now she could only remember the stolen moments with Will. Their kisses in the parlor downstairs. The feel of his body next to hers in her bedroom. The afternoons she'd sat in the conservatory, wondering if she would catch a glimpse of him passing through the garden. Her marriage and her husband had died in this house. But it was also the place where her love for Will had bloomed.

She was drawn out of her memories by a knock on the front door. She answered it and saw Winslow and Beatrice standing on the porch.

"Evelyn!" Winslow announced cheerfully, as if they were greeting each other at Sunday dinner. "Glad you're still here."

Beatrice was pressed against her father's side. She watched her aunt warily.

Evelyn leaned over and opened her arms, and Beatrice fell into them.

"Aunt Evelyn!" she said. "I miss you."

"I miss you, too," Evelyn said. "I'm so happy to see you." Standing up while keeping one arm around

Beatrice's shoulders, she said to Winslow, "Please come in."

Winslow looked quickly toward the front drive. "I'm afraid we don't have much time," he said. "It's Lavinia, you see. She wouldn't approve. I hope you understand."

Evelyn nodded.

"It's a secret!" Beatrice whispered, her eyes wide with excitement. "Daddy says I'm not to tell Mother we saw you!"

"How exciting," Evelyn said. "Secrets are fun, aren't they?"

"It's awfully awkward," Winslow said. "Lavinia feels bound to take her mother's side, though I think Alma has treated you most unfairly."

"It doesn't matter," Evelyn said, and she realized she meant it. Unlike Winslow, she no longer had to worry about living according to the Brewster code.

"In any case, you and Beatrice share a special bond," Winslow continued. "She deserves the chance to say goodbye."

Beatrice started crying, a few hiccups at first, then shuddering sobs. As Evelyn held the girl's shaking body, she began to cry, too. She'd thought she could make a clean break with the Brewsters, but part of her would always worry about Beatrice. How could she ever be happy, growing up in this family?

"Why do you have to leave?" Beatrice demanded.

Evelyn struggled to find a way to make her niece understand. "It makes me too sad, staying here," she said.

"But I love this house!" Beatrice said. "It's my favorite place in the whole world."

"Will you take care of it for me?" Evelyn asked.

"I'll write and tell you all about it," Beatrice agreed. "Will you write to me, too?"

Evelyn looked up at Winslow. He nodded.

"Once I'm settled," Evelyn said, "I'll send a letter with my address. I promise."

"Perhaps Aunt Evelyn should send her letter to me, at the office," Winslow suggested. "That way we can keep our secret."

"Ooh, yes," Beatrice said. "A secret correspondence! Like in a book!"

Evelyn brushed the tears from Beatrice's cheeks. "I promise I won't forget you." The diamond on her wedding ring flashed in the sunlight. Evelyn took the ring off and pressed it into Beatrice's hand. "Here," she said. "Something to remember me by."

"Are you sure?" Winslow asked.

"I don't need it anymore," Evelyn said.

"Where will you be going?" Winslow asked.

"California." Evelyn couldn't resist saying it aloud, feeling the way the letters rolled off her tongue.

"That's a long journey on your own!" Winslow protested. "Why ever would you feel the need…" His voice trailed off. At the same moment, Evelyn remembered something Will had said at the dinner table one evening, that if he had to live his life over again, he would start afresh in a place like California. Alma had accused him of being ridiculous, and Winslow had fretted about the unsavory types who settled in such remote areas. But Will had stood firm. Now, as Winslow looked at Evelyn, she blushed.

"Ah—I see, of course," he muttered. "Well, then, I hope you'll give him my best."

Evelyn nodded.

"Come," Winslow said to Beatrice, taking his daughter's arm. He reached into his coat pocket with his other hand. "Something for your journey," he said. Evelyn took the thick envelope imprinted with the Brewster Shipping address. Had Charles left some sort of document for her at the office?

"What is this?" Evelyn asked, but Winslow shook his head.

"Save it for later," he said. "Thank you for everything you've done for Beatrice." He turned to his daughter. "Come now."

Beatrice hugged and kissed Evelyn one last time before being gently pulled away by her father. Evelyn watched Winslow lean down and talk to Beatrice as they made their way along the drive. Winslow might be pompous and boring, but he was a good father. Perhaps, with him, Beatrice stood a chance.

Evelyn didn't have time to open the envelope after they left. She was already late for lunch at her mother's house, where she planned to spend the day before leaving for good. She slid the envelope into one of her bags, and it wasn't until the next day, when she'd taken her seat on the train to Chicago, that she thought to open it. Inside, she found no documents and no letter. Simply a stack of ten dollar bills. Evelyn nervously shoved the money back into her bag, hoping no one had seen it. Peeking inside, she flipped through the bills. Winslow had given her a thousand dollars. Enough to begin a new life.

SHE AND WILL COUNTED the money again, over and over, on that first rapturous night together in San Francisco.

"Good old Winslow!" Will had exclaimed with a laugh. "Who ever thought I'd be saying that?"

Already, there was something different about Will. The burden of the Brewster reputation had been lifted, thrown off like a scratchy, suffocating overcoat. Will's face, always cheerful but calm, now lit up when he smiled, which he did almost continuously from the moment he spotted Evelyn in the hotel lobby. He'd introduced her to the desk clerk as his wife, then hurried her up the stairs to his room, kissing her neck and making her giggle with embarrassment and pleasure. His happiness was infectious.

Their reunion upstairs was quick and intense. Freed from the fear of being caught, they came together with breathless relief. Afterward, they lay entwined, eagerly making plans for the future.

"We'll pay him back," Will said.

"Of course we will," Evelyn said. "Once we get settled."

"Speaking of which," Will said. He reached over to the bedside table and picked up a small velvet drawstring bag. "This is for you."

Evelyn pulled out a ring—a simple silver band.

"It's not much," Will said. "Nothing to compare to that diamond Charles gave you. Still, I was hoping…"

Evelyn slid the ring on her finger. It fit perfectly.

"Yes," Evelyn said with a smile. "I would be honored to be your wife."

They were married a few days later in a quiet courthouse ceremony, with the judge's secretary as their witness. Evelyn wore a pale pink dress that Will had suggested she buy on one of their shopping trips to Baltimore a lifetime ago. They used some of Winslow's money to buy a five-course meal in the hotel's dining room, complete with champagne.

"To us," Will said, raising his glass in a toast.

"To starting over," Evelyn replied, clinking her glass against his.

With that, they turned their backs on the past. For years, as they slowly built new lives, they never spoke of the house in Oak Hill or what had happened on the roof that terrible afternoon. Until, one day, a figure from their past reappeared to remind them of what they'd left behind.

CHAPTER NINETEEN

LOGICALLY, ALISSA knew it was a mistake to date someone you worked with. She used to shake her head disapprovingly when she heard about office relationships, predicting they could only end badly. How could you possibly concentrate on your job when you were constantly distracted by your new crush and worrying about how you looked?

But that was before she met Danny. He had a way of tackling obstacles that would have defeated anyone else. Confronted with structural challenges in a building, he doggedly found a way to fix them without getting frustrated. He handled Alissa's concerns the same way, moving easily from coworker to boyfriend as the occasion demanded. He did it all so smoothly that Alissa wondered what she'd been so worried about.

During the day, Danny focused on the house. He greeted Alissa with a brief kiss each morning, then went right to work. As she installed wood blinds in the living room or painted the master bedroom, she could hear him hammering or sawing somewhere, but they wouldn't speak for hours. Over lunch, the conversation stayed strictly business, discussing their progress and upcoming projects.

Come evening, the dynamic changed. Danny courted Alissa with old-fashioned sweetness, asking her out on dinner dates or trips to the local bowling alley. He introduced her to his mother and his closest friends. He spent occasional nights over at the house, and she missed him when he didn't. It was very serious very soon and it felt right.

Only occasionally did they allow their feelings to get in the way of work. One afternoon, Alissa asked Danny to look at her clogged-up bathroom sink. Although he wasn't a plumber, he said he could probably clear the drain easily enough. While trying to loosen a rusty bolt under the sink with his wrench, he pulled off a weak section of pipe, spraying water all over the bathroom floor and soaking himself.

Alissa shrieked with surprise, then laughter, as Danny crammed the pipe back on while being pelted with water.

"Thanks a lot," he said sarcastically after the spray had been tamed. He pushed his dripping hair off his face.

"I'm sorry," Alissa said, still giggling. "It was like a cartoon."

"I'm a mess," Danny said. He took off his T-shirt and wrung it out in the sink. Alissa brought him her bath towel and wrapped it around his shoulders. Before she could move away, Danny dropped the T-shirt and grabbed her.

"Was this part of your evil plan?" he asked. "A wet T-shirt contest?"

Alissa leaned toward him, feeling the solidity of his body press against hers.

"Yes," she said.

"So you could have your way with me?"

Alissa smiled. Danny's hands moved from her waist down along her hips. Drips of water from his hair fell onto her neck.

The doorbell rang downstairs.

"Oh, no," Alissa said. She'd completely forgotten. Elaine, her Realtor, had asked if she could bring someone over to see the renovated house, and Alissa had suggested this afternoon. She backed away from Danny and gave him an apologetic smile.

"It's Elaine and her friend. I have to give them the house tour. I've got some old workout T-shirts in the dresser if you want something dry to wear."

She gave him a quick kiss, then hurried toward the stairs as the doorbell rang again.

Alissa arrived at the door flushed and distracted. She opened the door, trying to smile.

"Hello there!" Elaine said, immaculate as usual in a tweed suit and several pieces of elaborate gold jewelry. "Hope we're not catching you at a bad time."

"We were having some plumbing problems upstairs," Alissa said, "but Danny's got a handle on it." She turned to the woman at Elaine's side and held out her hand. "Hello, I'm Alissa Franklin."

"Melody Foster." Alissa was taken aback for a moment. So this was the woman who'd owned the house before her. She was taller than Alissa had expected, with straight shoulders and a brisk manner that gave her an air of authority. Her hand held Alissa's in a firm grip, but her smile was wide and warm. It was only after she came inside that Alissa saw an indication of her true age, as her shoes shuffled more than stepped into the foyer.

"Oh!" she exclaimed, looking up toward the ceiling.

"The chandelier?" Alissa asked. "It's lovely, isn't it?"

"I don't think I ever saw it sparkle like that," Melody said. "How beautiful."

"Well, cleaning it was quite a job, but it was worth it," Alissa said. "The rest of the house isn't quite so impressive, I'm afraid. It's still a work in progress."

Melody shook her head as she slowly turned around, taking everything in. "You were right," she said to Elaine. "She deserves this house."

Elaine nodded.

"Would you like to take a look around?" Alissa asked. "You might not recognize the kitchen."

As they started down the hallway to the dining room, Alissa heard Danny's work boots clattering down the stairs. Elaine waved at him.

"Hello, Danny!" she called out flirtatiously. "Melody, this is Danny Pierce. He's doing work on the house for Alissa." She gave Alissa a teasing glance. Thanks to Danny's mother, the whole town knew they were dating.

Danny was wearing one of Alissa's old college T-shirts. Big on her, it fit him snugly around the shoulders and chest. He was fidgeting self-consciously, but the effect was flattering. Alissa wished her guests had come later.

Danny lifted his hand in a quick greeting. "Nice to meet you. Hi, Elaine. Alissa, I'm going to run to the store to get some stuff for that sink, okay?"

Alissa nodded.

"Looks and talent. It's not often you find that in the same man," Elaine said after Danny closed the door behind him. "Plus, he's so kind. His mother is a lucky woman." She peered at Alissa. *You are, too*, her gaze seemed to say.

Alissa led her guests through the house, moving slowly to accommodate Melody's shaky legs. Although Alissa wondered if it was hard for her to see someone else take over her old home, Melody appeared delighted by the changes.

After the tour, Alissa invited the women to join her for tea in the living room. This room, at least, was close to how she had envisioned it, with comfortable cream-colored couches and armchairs arranged around a square rug with a pattern of green vines. The wood fireplace mantel had been stripped of its white paint and refinished to its original luster. The room felt both elegant and relaxed, the precise effect Alissa had hoped for.

"You lived here for a long time, didn't you?" Alissa asked. She already knew, thanks to her digging through the county records, that Melody Foster and her husband had bought the house in 1973.

"More than thirty years," Melody said. "After my husband died, my sister moved in to keep me company. We weren't able to maintain it the way I'd hoped, and it simply became too much for us." Alissa could hear the wistfulness in her voice. It couldn't have been easy to move from this gracious home to a retirement complex.

"I hope you'll come again," Alissa said. "We've got a lot more work to do, as you can see. And your sister, too, if she'd like."

"She's living with her daughter in Boston, but I'll tell her. She might like to come down. It's always been more than just a house to us."

"It does have a certain spirit, doesn't it?" Alissa asked. "I felt it the very first time I visited."

Melody smiled. "It's more than that to me. It's not something I've ever talked about, but I have a family connection to this place."

"Really?" Alissa asked. Elaine looked intrigued.

"The original owner was my grandmother," Melody said.

But that was impossible, Alissa thought. The original owners were Charles and Evelyn Brewster, and they never had children.

"You may have heard of Evelyn Brewster," Melody began.

Alissa nodded, and Elaine said, "Of course."

"I'm her granddaughter," Melody continued. "Her first husband died young, and she moved to California to marry his brother, Will. My grandfather."

Will? He'd barely been mentioned in the family records Alissa had read so thoroughly. She'd dismissed him as a minor character.

"I don't know much about my grandparents' lives before they moved to San Francisco," Melody said apologetically. "Although I gather their marriage would've been quite the scandal."

"I would say so!" Elaine exclaimed. "I never heard a thing about it!"

"Did she ever say anything about her first husband, Charles?" Alissa asked.

Melody shook her head. "All I know is what my

mother told me years later—that my grandparents once said they saved each other from a lifetime of misery."

"If you only knew how much time I've spent wondering about Evelyn and what happened to her!" Alissa marveled. "And now you're saying she lived happily ever after."

"Oh, yes," Melody said. "My grandfather ran a very successful business, importing artwork and furniture from Europe. My grandmother was one of those women who's always involved in some charity project or another. They had one child, my mother, and brought her up in a lovely house on the edge of Nob Hill. I grew up less than a mile away and spent every Sunday with them. Even when they were older and considerably slower, they had such a spark. I adored them."

"How did you end up here?" Alissa asked.

"As far as I know, my grandparents stayed in contact with only one person in the Brewster family, my cousin Beatrice. I met her once, when she visited California after the Second World War. I wish I could tell you more about her, but I was so young and quite uninterested in family history then. I remember her as reserved but kind. We found out later she was quite sick, and she died not long after. In her will, she left this house in some sort of trust for my mother. Beatrice had no children, you see, and she wanted the house to remain in the family."

Alissa remembered the courthouse records, the bank in San Francisco. Now she understood.

"My mother was understandably confused," Melody continued. "What did she want with a house in Maryland?

My grandparents insisted she see the house before deciding what to do with it. They paid for plane tickets and brought her here for a visit."

"Evelyn came back?" Alissa asked, excitement rising.

Melody nodded. "My sister and I were in school at the time, so we stayed in California with my father. I remember the fight my parents had when Mother returned from the trip and told Father she wouldn't sell the house. He'd assumed they would, of course, and then there she was, putting her foot down and saying no. They eventually compromised and made arrangements to rent it out.

"Still, I grew up thinking the house would be sold sooner or later. It certainly didn't mean anything to me. Eventually, through a long series of events I won't bore you with, my husband was offered a teaching position at the University of Maryland. I can't help seeing it now as an act of fate. Suddenly, here we were, moving to the area where my mother happened to own a house. For tax reasons, my parents decided to sell us the house for a very reasonable amount rather than give it to us. Alissa, I think you'll understand when I tell you I fell in love with the place immediately.

"I always hoped one of my daughters would want to live here someday, but neither of them wanted the responsibility of this old place. Once I accepted I'd have to sell it, I told Elaine I'd wait for the right person. The money wasn't important—I wanted someone who would treasure this house as much as I did. And then you came along."

"In all the time you lived here, why didn't you ever tell anyone you were related to the Brewsters?" Elaine demanded.

"Soon after I moved in, I realized the Brewster name still had a powerful mystique," Melody explained. "I wanted to raise my family in peace. I certainly didn't want anyone thinking I'd inherited a fortune!"

"Shame on you," Elaine said teasingly.

Melody turned to Alissa. "Elaine told me you've been quite taken with the home's history," she said. "I thought you might be interested in seeing a picture of my grandparents." She reached into her bag and pulled out a sepia-toned photograph. It showed a young couple standing close together, holding hands. Alissa recognized Evelyn immediately. Her dark hair, pulled in waves on the top of her head, looked the same as it had in other pictures, but her expression was one Alissa had never seen. She was smiling happily, exuding a warmth that brightened her whole face. Next to her, Will Brewster had the same piercing eyes as his brother, but none of Charles's cool detachment. Will was undeniably handsome, but he wore his good looks loosely, without self-consciousness.

Will and Evelyn looked at Alissa across the years. They felt as real to her as Melody and Elaine a few feet away. She thought of the picture of Charles and Evelyn in their party finery, sitting forlornly in an upstairs bedroom. She knew she wouldn't keep it. She would make a copy of this one instead, showing a happy Brewster couple. Theirs was the spirit she wanted to celebrate in this house.

The front door opened and Danny walked in. As he strolled into the living room, Alissa was overwhelmed by a rush of emotion. Is this how Evelyn had felt, watching Will Brewster? Knowing he was the last person she should fall in love with, but unable to resist?

Alissa waved to Danny, motioning him to join them in the living room.

"Danny—there's a story you have to hear." She patted the sofa next to her. She wanted him to hear the story of Will and Evelyn Brewster. She wanted him to know that happy endings were possible.

EPILOGUE

"Two years?" Constance asked. "Really?"

"Almost exactly," Alissa said. Two years since she'd bought what she still thought of as the Brewster house. Two years in which she'd transformed her entire life. Two years of uncertainty, frustration, excitement and passion. And, at last, contentment.

"I never imagined you'd get a husband out of the deal," Constance said. She followed Alissa through the French doors in the kitchen and out to the patio, where a row of glazed blue planters brightened the stark expanse of stone.

"Remember when Danny first came for the interview?" Alissa laughed. "We thought he'd be some old guy missing half his teeth."

"And he turned out to be the hunky handyman!" Constance said.

"I remember—I was so annoyed at you," Alissa mused. "Flirting with him when I was trying to be all professional. Dating was the last thing on my mind."

"That's why it worked out. Good things happen when you least expect them."

"For you, too," Alissa reminded her friend.

She looked at the little boy galloping across the lawn

ahead of them. When Constance had signed up to be a foster mother, she had expected a short-term placement, a crash course in parenting to prepare for when she finally got pregnant. But Constance had fallen in love with two-year-old Ty immediately, showering him with the love she had hoarded for so many years. When Ty's mother, unable to overcome her heroin addiction, begged the social workers to take the child off her hands, Constance had offered to adopt him. The child she'd dreamed of for so long hadn't arrived the way she'd imagined, but he was hers nonetheless.

Getting Ty had prompted a few other changes in Constance's life. In order to spend more time with her son, she quit her job and decided to join forces with Alissa. The new offices of Franklin, Powers and Pierce—a full-service renovation and design firm with Constance as architect, Alissa as designer and Danny as contractor—had recently been set up in the old conservatory.

Danny and Alissa had made their personal partnership official a few months before, exchanging vows in a simple ceremony followed by an informal reception at home. Close friends and family celebrated with dancing in the foyer well into the night. They'd decided to put off the honeymoon to focus on finishing the house, but Danny was already dropping hints about the European itinerary he was planning for next year.

"Ty! Stop!" Constance scolded. The boy turned to her, brandishing the daffodils he'd pulled from the flower beds.

"It's all right," Alissa said. "We're going to redo all this anyway. Go ahead, Ty—you can keep playing."

"Are you boring Constance with your latest To Do list?" Danny stepped out from the kitchen holding a pitcher of lemonade and a stack of plastic cups.

"Not at all," Constance protested, taking a cup from Danny and holding it out for him to fill. "What do you have planned?"

"Alissa wants to open all this up," Danny explained. "Tear out the hedges, put down sod."

"It would be a lot easier to maintain," Alissa pointed out.

"It would also mean ripping out my favorite part of the yard," Danny said in a resigned tone that signaled this was a frequent, unresolved topic of conversation.

Constance looked at Alissa questioningly.

"Haven't you seen it?" Alissa asked. She led the way to the garden room and Danny and Constance followed, holding Ty's hands, through the opening in the hedges. New leaves had started to fill in the branches of the maple tree above them.

"Oh, this is charming!" Constance exclaimed. "Your own private getaway."

"See?" Danny put one arm around Alissa's shoulders and held the other hand out toward Constance.

"It's like *The Secret Garden*," Constance said. "You remember that book, don't you?"

"It would be a shame to lose this tree," Danny said.

"I'd keep the tree," Alissa said. "Just pull out the hedges and plantings. And get rid of this old seat."

Ty was squatting at the side of the bench, his fingers tracing along the stone. Danny leaned over next to him.

"Have you seen these?" he asked.

Alissa crouched down to take a look. The bench was a simple, flat slab of stone, mounted on two rectangular pieces for legs. The sides were carved with an intricate pattern of vines and branches. Like Ty, Alissa couldn't resist reaching out and feeling the curves of the vegetation. It was a shame that such skilled work had been wasted here, in a part of the garden where no one ever saw it.

Danny pointed to a few marks at the very edge of the seat. From a distance, they looked like random scrapes. But staring at them up close, Alissa could make out some letters.

"Emy?" Danny sounded out. "That doesn't make any sense."

Tiny particles of stone had fallen away over the years, making the letters jagged and hard to decipher. It must have taken some effort to carve them into such dense material.

Alissa traced the lines with her finger. She felt a slightly wider space between the *E* and the *m* and *y*. Separate words. Carefully, she looked for a pattern. Then the markings clicked into place.

E. My love. W.

Evelyn. William. They'd been here.

How many times had she sat here, Alissa wondered, within inches of these letters, and not seen them? How had this simple declaration of love survived a hundred years of rain and snow and sun?

Then Alissa remembered that Will and Evelyn had returned to the house once, many years later. Will, by then a grandfather, could have sat here, painstakingly declaring his love for the woman who shared his life. This place must have meant something to them.

Alissa took Danny's hand and traced his finger over the initials. She watched his eyes widen as he took in the significance of the letters.

"Danny, you're right," she said. "Let's keep it just like this."

"Good call," he agreed.

"I have to tell Colin to carve our initials somewhere," Constance said. "It's so romantic—Ty!" She jumped up and raced after her son, who'd sprinted back out to the lawn. Their laughter filtered through the hedges. Alissa sat quietly on the grass beside the bench as Danny settled down beside her.

"Thinking about the Brewsters again?" Danny asked.

"Yeah. I think they'd be happy we're here."

"I think you're right."

They sat nestled together, fingers entwined, as Will and Evelyn had so many years before, listening to the wind rustle through the leaves above them.

* * * * *

*Celebrate 60 years of pure reading pleasure
with Harlequin®!*

*Step back in time and enjoy a sneak preview of an
exciting anthology from Harlequin® Historical with
THE DIAMONDS OF WELBOURNE MANOR*

This compelling anthology features three stories
about the outrageous Fitzmanning sisters. Meet
Annalise, who is never at a loss for words… But
that can change with an unexpected encounter in
the forest.

Available May 2009 from Harlequin® Historical.

"I'm the illegitimate daughter of notoriously scandalous parents, Mr. Milford. Candidates for my hand are unlikely to be lining up at the gates."

"Don't be so quick to discount your charms, my dear. Or the charm of your substantial dowry. Or even your brothers' influence. There are as many reasons to marry as there are marriages."

Annalise snorted. "Oh, yes. Perhaps I shall marry for dynastic reasons, or perhaps for property or influence. After all, a loveless, practical marriage worked out so well for my mother."

"Well, you've routed me on that one. I can think of no suitable rejoinder." Ned rose to his feet and extended his hand. "And since that is the case, let me be the first to wish you a long and happy spinsterhood."

Her mouth gaped open. And then she laughed.

And he froze.

This was the first time, Ned realized. The first time he'd seen her eyes light up and her mouth curl. The first time he'd witnessed her features melded together in glorious accord to produce exquisite beauty.

Unbelievable what a change came over her face. Unheard of what effect her throaty, rasping laughter

248 The Diamonds of Welbourne Manor

had on his body. It pounded a beat upon his ear, quickly taken up by his pulse. It echoed through him, finally residing in his stirring nether regions.

So easily she did it, awakened these sensations within him—without any apparent effort at all. And she had called him potentially dangerous? Clearly the intelligent thing for him to do would be to steer clear, to leave her to the tender ministrations of Lord Peter Blackthorne.

"You were right." She smiled up at him as she took his hand and climbed to her feet. "I do feel better."

Ah, well. When had he ever chosen the intelligent path?

He did not relinquish her hand. He used it to pull her in, close enough that he could feel the warmth of her. "At the risk of repeating Lord Peter's mistake and anticipating too much—may I ask if you'll be my partner in battledore tomorrow?"

Her smiled dimmed. Her breath came a little faster. His own had gone shallow, as if he'd just run a race—and lost. He ran his gaze over the appealing lift of her brow and the curious angle of her chin. His index finger twitched.

"I should like that," she said.

His finger trembled again and he lifted it, traced the pink and tender shell of her ear, the unique sweep of her jaw. Her pulse leaped beneath her skin, triggering his own. Slowly he tilted her chin up, waiting for her to object, to step back, to slap his hand away.

She did none of those eminently sensible things. Which left him free to do the entirely impractical thing.

Baby soft, the skin of her lips. Her whole body trembled when he touched her there.

He leaned in. Her eyes closed, even as she stood straight against him, strung as tight as a bow. He pressed his mouth to hers. It was a soft kiss, sweet and chaste. And yet he was hot and hard and as ready as he'd ever been in his life.

She drew back a little. Sighed. Their breath mingled a moment before she slowly backed away.

"Oh," she breathed. Her dark eyes were full of wonder and something that looked like fear. He took a step toward her, but she only shook her head. His outstretched hand fell to his side as she turned to disappear into the wood. This was the first time, Ned realized. The first time, since he'd come to the house party at Welbourne Manor, that he'd seen her eyes light up.

* * * * *

Follow Ned and Annalise's story in May 2009 in
THE DIAMONDS OF WELBOURNE MANOR
Available May 2009 from Harlequin® Historical

Available in the series romance section,
or in the historical romance section,
wherever books are sold.

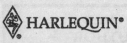

HARLEQUIN®

American ★ Romance®

LAURA MARIE ALTOM
The Marine's Babies

Men Made in America

Captain Jace Monroe is everything a Marine
should be—strong, brave and honorable. He's also
an instant father of twin baby girls he never knew
existed! Life gets even more complicated when he
finds himself attracted to Emma Stewart, his new
nanny. But can this sexy, fun-loving bachelor do
the right thing and become a family man?
Emma and the babies are counting on it!

**Available in May
wherever books are sold.**

LOVE, HOME & HAPPINESS

Our

ON BOARD
miniseries has grown!

Now you can share in even more
tears and triumphs as
Harlequin Romance® brings you
a month full of

Pregnancy and Proposals,
Miracles and Marriage!

*Available in May
wherever books are sold.*

REQUEST YOUR FREE BOOKS!

2 FREE NOVELS PLUS 2 FREE GIFTS!

HARLEQUIN®

Super Romance®

Exciting, emotional, unexpected!

YES! Please send me 2 FREE Harlequin® Superromance® novels and my 2 FREE gifts (gifts are worth about $10). After receiving them, if I don't wish to receive any more books, I can return the shipping statement marked "cancel." If I don't cancel, I will receive 6 brand-new novels every month and be billed just $4.69 per book in the U.S. or $5.24 per book in Canada. That's a savings of close to 15% off the cover price! It's quite a bargain! Shipping and handling is just 25¢ per book*. I understand that accepting the 2 free books and gifts places me under no obligation to buy anything. I can always return a shipment and cancel at any time. Even if I never buy another book from Harlequin, the two free books and gifts are mine to keep forever.

135 HDN EEX7   336 HDN EEYK

Name	(PLEASE PRINT)	
Address		Apt. #
City	State/Prov.	Zip/Postal Code

Signature (if under 18, a parent or guardian must sign)

Mail to the Harlequin Reader Service:
IN U.S.A.: P.O. Box 1867, Buffalo, NY 14240-1867
IN CANADA: P.O. Box 609, Fort Erie, Ontario L2A 5X3

Not valid to current subscribers of Harlequin Superromance books.

**Are you a current subscriber of Harlequin Superromance books and want to receive the larger-print edition?
Call 1-800-873-8635 today!**

* Terms and prices subject to change without notice. Prices do not include applicable taxes. Sales tax applicable in N.Y. Canadian residents will be charged applicable provincial taxes and GST. Offer not valid in Quebec. This offer is limited to one order per household. All orders subject to approval. Credit or debit balances in a customer's account(s) may be offset by any other outstanding balance owed by or to the customer. Please allow 4 to 6 weeks for delivery. Offer available while quantities last.

Your Privacy: Harlequin is committed to protecting your privacy. Our Privacy Policy is available online at www.eHarlequin.com or upon request from the Reader Service. From time to time we make our lists of customers available to reputable third parties who may have a product or service of interest to you. If you would prefer we not share your name and address, please check here. ☐

HSR09

HARLEQUIN Super Romance

COMING NEXT MONTH

Available May 12, 2009

#1560 SUMMER AT THE LAKE • Linda Barrett
Count on a Cop
This lakeside cabin is the perfect place for Kristin McCarthy and her daughter to piece together their lives. But with Kristin's distrust of cops, who would have thought one—namely Rick Cooper—would help her daughter heal? Or that Kristin would fall for him?

#1561 HE CALLS HER DOC • Mary Brady
To prove to her hometown that she's good enough to be its doctor, Maude DeVane needs time. And she has it. Until Guy Daley—the doctor she once thought she loved—shows up. She can't seem to avoid him, especially when his niece turns matchmaker!

#1562 THE STRANGER'S SIN • Darlene Gardner
Return to Indigo Springs
Wrongfully accused of a crime, Kelly Carmichael has no choice but to solve the case. That brings her to Indigo Springs and the attentions of park ranger Chase Bradford. A special bond quickly forms between them, but will it survive what they discover?

#1563 THE BOYFRIEND'S BACK • Ellen Hartman
Going Back
As a pregnant teen, letting everyone believe JT McNulty was the father of her child seemed the only answer to Hailey Maddox's predicament. But she never guessed the impact her lie would have. And now, after all these years, JT's come home....

#1564 PICTURE-PERFECT MOM • Debra Salonen
Spotlight on Sentinel Pass
It's a TV plot. What are the odds of Mac McGannon falling for a star like Morgana Carlyle? Yeah, that slim. But it's happening. And he's not the only one. His daughter thinks Morgana is the perfect mom. Just one snag—Morgana is not who she claims to be.

#1565 WEDDINGS IN THE FAMILY• Tessa McDermid
Everlasting Love
On the day of their daughter's wedding, Caroline questions her own marriage to Nick. Facing life's ups and downs, she expected they'd be closer than ever. But he seems so far away from her now. After a lifetime together, can they find the love they once shared?

HSRCNMBPA0409